John Hill

The Common Ancestor

Vol. III

John Hill

The Common Ancestor
Vol. III

ISBN/EAN: 9783337052843

Printed in Europe, USA, Canada, Australia, Japan

Cover: Foto ©Andreas Hilbeck / pixelio.de

More available books at **www.hansebooks.com**

THE COMMON ANCESTOR

A Novel

BY

JOHN HILL

AUTHOR OF 'TREASON-FELONY,' ETC.

IN THREE VOLUMES

VOL. III.

London

CHATTO & WINDUS, PICCADILLY

1894

THE COMMON ANCESTOR

CHAPTER XXII.

In the afternoon the two Scanlans were
taken by their guide or shepherd (or keeper,
as Dick suggested) for their first walk in a
foreign town, in warm sunshine and cloudless
weather. It is needless to dwell on the manner
in which they spent the time, as nearly every-
one has had to pass a day or half a day in
Cologne at some time of his or her existence,
and they all do much the same things,
beginning with the Cathedral and the Three
Kings, and then going over the iron Kaiser-
brücke to see the Rhine, passing along the
Deutz side as far as the bridge of boats,
coming back over the latter (which haply

comes in two when they are half-way over)
and landing below the old tavern with
' Zum Vater Rhein ' in big black letters on
its white gable facing the river, to walk up
among the old squares and statues and
follow the little curling tram-line back to
the middle of the town.   Then photographs
and the inevitable Farina water, followed by
fatigue and rest.   All this they did, and
were delighted, Nora more especially with
the Cathedral, Dick with the river and the
numerous white Cuirassiers and dark-blue
linesmen who pervaded the place, and the
occasional strapping square-shouldered, tight-
legged officers in long - skirted, narrow-
waisted coats, and both with the utter
unfamiliarity of aspect of everything, build-
ings, pavements, atmosphere, and human
beings.   They were introduced to Lieb-
fraumilch in the evening at dinner, and their
respect for Cunningham's attainments was
heightened by the apparent ease with which
he spoke a language to them a hopeless
jargon.

'Never mind,' said Dick after dinner, when they had strolled out for a look at the Rhine by night and a cigar ; ' I'm going to learn Jorman. They are a fine lot, and properly drilled, not like those miserable guttersnipes we saw in Holland this morning, and I'd be proud to speak with 'em and take a glass of that beer with a German sergeant-major or two. We should cotton first class.'

' I believe you would,' said Cunningham ; ' we'll try some time or other.'

' Dick 'll never forget his barricks, I think,' said Nora.

' Dick will not, and you may take your oath of that, me lady,' said the cheery ex-Grenadier with a gentle smile.

It was fortunate that Dick was extremely good-tempered and patient, so that any little impulsive flouts on the part of his kindly but rather ' touchy ' sister were simply as stones dropped into a soft mud-bank.

Next morning Cunningham was awakened

early by Dick, in white flannel trousers, a
buttoned-up tweed jacket concealing a total
absence of collar, and his Tam-o'-Shanter, who
wished to know whether a 'bit of a swim'
was practicable. Cunningham said it un-
doubtedly was, though a trifle chilly at that
time of day and year, got up hastily, and
valiantly accompanied Dick to the Rhine
bath, where they took icy headers and returned to the dry land with blue hands and
lips, which, however, very shortly assumed
their normal condition in the morning sunshine. Dick lit his little black pipe, pulled
out his watch, as they walked back to the
hotel, and compared it with the clocks he
heard striking eight.

'I suppose Nora's asleep?'

'Divil doubt her! She's the fine girl for
sleeping.'

'You've the fine tongue for lying, Dick,'
observed the lady mentioned, who was
standing at the doorway of the hotel (near
which the above sentences were exchanged),
in a light tailor-made homespun, the colour

of *thé-au-lait*, which indicated that her trunk had been requisitioned to provide for the change of climate. When they left London the day before yesterday, it was almost winter. To-day, in Rhineland, it was almost summer. It is not always so at that season, but our travellers were very fortunate.

'We had better take advantage of this weather to get southward,' observed Cunningham ; 'Cologne here is only a sort of junction, which nearly everybody has to pass through ; but there is nothing more here to see and do than you have seen and done.'

'Give us the route,' said Dick, 'and we'll be ready. Let me see,' he added, consulting his timepiece again, 'it's ten minutes past eight now. Well, what time ought we to go, any way ?'

'The station's close by. There's a train about half-past nine. If you will go and pack up, I will order breakfast and get the bill, and we will do very well.'

The two orphans departed, chasing each
other upstairs like schoolboys.

Soon they were at the station, looked on
at the ticket-buying and luggage-weighing
with intelligent curiosity, and were taken
along the platform to a long, long train with
all the doors open—doors with wooden
linings, doors with drab-gray cloth linings,
doors with red velvet linings. They chose
the drab-gray variety, as Cunningham had
pointed out that the first-class was a use-
less extravagance, and that the red velvet
made one hot to look at.

Then they rolled away along the grand
old Rhine, through the little quiet old riverside towns, with their crumbling brown walls
and creeper-clad gardens mellowing with
autumn colour, and their inevitable pink or
yellow-fronted *Gasthaus-zum-Anker*; past
the vine-covered mountain-sides, the castled
peaks, the islets with solitary convents or
towers, the Lorelei-Fels, where Cunningham told the legend, and promised to teach
Nora the song as soon as they came to a

place where there was a piano; past the
Pfalzgrafenstein and long, green, flat islands
into red, episcopal Mainz, with its fine new
station ; across the river by the bridge,
whose twinkling iron tracery dazzles the
eye and obstructs the view ; through fir-
clad plains and valleys to Darmstadt, in
which highly-respectable but depressing
town they took mid-day dinner—which you
may be sure Dick was ready for—on to
Asschaffenburg, where a dear old bright-
blue Bavarian guard with a silver lanyard
took them in charge, and treated them like
old friends ; and on through Bavarian fields
and forests, where the wayside crucifixes
and stations reminded them a little of Ireland, to Würzburg on the Main, with the
picturesque Marienberg citadel, and the
high, bare-looking hills, where the good
Leisten-wine grows. Here they made a
halt for the night, after their stage-coach
manner of travelling. As Cunningham
said :

' We are not in any desperate hurry.

We want to be comfortable, and, above all,
we want to see the places : so it seemed to
me we had better stop here for the night.
There can be no possible fun in spending a
long, dark, and probably chilly night in a
train when we are not obliged, and this
place came just at the right time, when we
had had our fair dose of train.'

This remark he made while they were all
three joggling over the pavement of the
homely little Bavarian town in a *droschke*,
with the ponderous house-boy of an inn
sitting on Nora's trunk alongside the driver,
and making conspicuous dents in it. They
went to an old *Hof* in the market-place,
with large arched windows and doorway on
the ground-floor, and queer, dark staircase
leading into slippery tiled passages all on a
slant ; upstairs, where they were shown into
rooms which looked out on to the wide
market, now deserted, but to be filled early
next morning with a dense crowd of women
encamped under white umbrellas, and reposing on heaps of vegetables and country

produce of different kinds, among whom housewives and servants with baskets would circulate, with an occasional policeman to drop his hydrometer into the milk-cans, and mercilessly upset any irrigated milk into the gutter, and all—market-women, housewives, hens, policemen, ducks and geese—making the most tremendous gabble and cackle together in the morning sunshine.

'I like this part of the country,' said Dick. 'It's out of the way of the world, and the people are pleasant and friendly-looking, and seem to take life very easy. There's something about them that makes me think of Ireland.'

'Bayerisch rather suggests Irish, perhaps,' replied Cunningham.

They were all taking a stroll about the quaint old town, which, be it remarked, is the easiest one in all the world to lose your way in when a comparative stranger. That is the strong point of Würzburg. They penetrated the rather pleasant, fragrant gardens attached to the Residence, a vast

and ornate but dreary, yellowish building,
in the inevitable eighteenth-century French
style peculiar to Residences, and looked at
the views from the terraces. Then they
came back into the winding Würzburg
streets, and proceeded to lose themselves
twice before arriving at their inn. The
evening was spent in supper (baked carp
and potatoes, with the wine called Innere
Leiste), and cosy conversation, with smoke,
and friendly attempts at conversation on
the part of the boy who had dented the
trunk, who appeared to keep the hotel—a
very polite boy, with dark eyes and white
teeth and an amiable smile, who told them
what they ought to do and asked them what
they had done.

' What's that he says ?' said Nora.

' He is cross-examining me on the various
sights, and doesn't mean to let me off anything, so I am assuring him that we have
minutely examined all the churches without
exception, and the tomb of Walther von der
Vogelweide, who was a mediæval minstrel,

about whom I don't think we feel anxious.
But would you like to go up and see the
Marienberg to-morrow morning? It's
rather picturesque and antique, and there's
a splendid view.'

'It looks fine from below,' said Dick,
'and that's what most high things do.'

'You lazy creature!' said Nora ; 'it's the
walking you're afraid of. Of course we'll
be delighted to go up there.'

'I didn't propose that we should walk,'
replied Cunningham.

After explanations, which appeared to
gratify the boy, Cunningham continued :

'He assures me in the best Bayerisch
brogue, with singing vowels and all his final
" n's " left out, that the best *droschke* in
Würzburg will await our commands immediately after breakfast.'

'There's the river here, what's its name ?'
said Dick.

'The Main—yes ?'

'Can we get into it before breakfast ?'

'Oh yes. You wake me up, and the boy

will tell us the way. Sure to be a swim-bath.' And the obliging boy left them, to entertain other guests.

'Homely old place, isn't it?' said Cunning-ham. 'I mean homely in English, not in the American sense; and it does very well to break the journey, and I thought you might be interested to see how the people live in an old-world Bavarian town.'

'It's very interesting, I think,' said Nora. 'I like it all very much. I do indeed now. And I think you are managing our travel-ling beautifully.'

'Just think now,' said Dick, 'what a man must know, to be able to work along in this smooth way, with no trouble to anyone, and talking the languages and all, and going to the right places, and knowing the kind of things to ask for and how to get the right side of the people—look at the way he blarneyed that boy and sent him away smiling.'

'Look at the way you are blarneying me, my boy, if it comes to that. It's only a matter of habit and opportunity, *plus* ordinary intelligence.'

'Well, I wish I had your education, Cunningham, that's all.'

'Man! It *is* education to do what you're doing now, just as it was education to be in the army, and an education better than a good many others. Besides, you are very well educated in the more restricted sense of the word, much more so than many a " tenth transmitter of a foolish face" who has been to a university, and held a commission, and played baccarat, or kept racehorses, or entertained chorus-girls and sporting journalists, and all the rest of the ruck of parasites that hang on to a fool till he and his money are parted. Learn not to undervalue yourself. People in this world—I don't know much about the other worlds—will usually take you at your own price. They value goods by the label or the advertisement. If you tell them a true thing, quietly, they won't believe it; but you shout it loud and shout it often, and placard it on walls and omnibuses, and they will believe it, even if it be an untrue thing. Cheek's the winner in the modern race for success.'

' Bedad, there's a deal of sense in that.' And Dick went upstairs to fetch his tobacco-pouch.

' I never knew you speak so much as if you meant it before, Mr. Cunningham. You generally talk as if it was really too much trouble to be in earnest about anything. I don't mean in what you do, you take plenty of trouble about that—and if it's doing kind things for other people you take all the more. But when I first knew you I didn't like you at all, because you talked as if you were *just* amusing yourself with people and kept a serious face merely for outward show and civility.'

'You know better now, I hope ?'

' Oh yes.   I understand you more now.'

' That's all right.'

Dick returned, saying :

' What time do we go to-morrow ?   That is, I suppose we *do* go to-morrow ?'

'Yes, I think so. We'll get to the capital of Bavaria to-morrow. To-morrow's Saturday, and we might do well to stay there till Monday. We leave here about mid-day.'

'Sure you're a walking time-table! Then, if we're going up to the citadel there after breakfast, we'd breakfast at eight, I suppose?'

'Well, yes, I suppose so.'

'Then, Nora, you'd better go to bed soon. It's hard on ten, and you want a good rest.'

'Well, then, I think I will. Good-night, Mr. Cunningham.'

'Good-night, Nora,' he said, shaking the firm, shapely hand which was offered him, and then watched her kiss Dick with the reflection, 'He's only her brother, and perhaps looks on the ceremony as rather a bore than otherwise.'

'Now, don't you boys be late,' was her parting shot. Cunningham sat down and continued to smile, like the gentleman in the rhyme who hoped to soften the heart of a ruminant. Dick, standing up before the stove in the picturesque old lamp-lit, arched *Gast-Stube* like some stalwart trumpeter or man-at-arms in a seventeenth-century picture taking his ease in his inn, packed his pipe with a fine dark seaweedy substance, and observed :

'Don't you think that decent lad would get us another bottle of that wine, if we put the idea into his head ?'

' It's not unlikely.   I'll try.'

*   *   *   *   *

The next evening, having passed many an ancient Bavarian village nestling in a sheltered hollow, where the brown high-peaked gables and the white tall church tower with bulbous ruddy spire alone showed among the tree-tops, or standing in the level far away in the misty distance of wide sunlit plains, the wanderers came in sight of the fortifications of Ingolstadt, in the saffron and daffodil afterglow, with a pure blue above dappled with radiant rosy clouds, becoming maddery-brown streaks as they approached the dusky reddening-yellow of the horizon, where the plains fringed and mingled with the sky, the far-off webs of foliage and the nearer solitary trees being, as it were, steeped in the sunset glow, instead of standing clear against it to assert that earth and heaven were never in coalescence, always in collision.

And later on, in the moonlight of a motionless autumn night, they came into the royal town of fairy-palaces, of green romantic parks, of neighbouring beautiful, sad, and mysterious lakes, where passed away, like Arthur, that mystic and wonderful monarch, the maker of splendour, the solitary star-lit poet of the midnight fir-crowned mountain paths, the worshipper of music who made a magnificent house for the wildest, maddest and most memorable music of the world, the innocent fairy-king whom men called mad, whose madness was more glorious than most men's sanity.

When, after rest and supper in the large cheery *Restauration-Saal* of the hotel, where gods and goddesses ' rampaged ' in weird

frescoes on the walls above them, and the
Münchener Kellnerins ran about with arm-
fuls of Seidels and piles of *Sauerbraten* and
Kopfsalat all round them, they went out
for a quiet stroll, and were standing on
the bridge over the white torrent of the
Isar.

That night Cunningham told them the
story of that strange, already legendary royal
life and death, that meteor descending to the
silent waters to be quenched, or to dwell
with Hamlet, with Lear, and with Arthur
for ever, till Tannhäuser be set free from
the Venusberg, till old Barbarossa and his
knights awake.

This girl and her brother were the best
people in the world whom Cunningham
could have chosen as listeners to that story,
who would understand the *märchenhaft*
beauty and sadness of it, for it touched
that string in the Irish harp which is
sweetest and strongest, and we hope will
live unbroken the longest, which is known
to those who know, and cannot be explained

to those who do not. A Highlander would understand it, too.

'It is beautiful, but it makes one shiver,' said Nora, looking at the resistless rush of the Isar, 'and I wouldn't have missed it for anything. Sure, this river's alive and singing to us ; and those dark trees along the other side are listening. Let us go home, now.'

'Cunningham,' said Dick, as they walked homewards along the Maximilian Strasse, "I wonder you don't write some stories instead of wasting your time over dry old rubbish in the philosophy line.'

'Perhaps I might try, now I am in the right sort of atmosphere ; but I was feeling dry and old myself when you found me worrying at the Individual and the Clan and all that, so the work was by way of appropriate.'

'I believe you could write splendid stories if you tried,' said Nora.

'And, after all, I suppose people will behave exactly the same whether I write Ethics for them or not.'

'Divil doubt 'em,' said Dick reassuringly.

'I suppose it is true, after all, that the songs and stories have moved and shaken the world more than all the philosophers. Besides, the philosophers are just the people to spoil the stories as soon as they get tinkering with them, and comparing, and classifying, and finding the Mother Goose myth in Patagonia in a new form, and all that sort of thing.'

'The Irish peasants will forget their stories soon,' said Dick, 'because, as soon as they've got what they call educated, they read nothing but newspapers, and talk about progress and politics, and nationalization of land, and then they get ashamed of the old stories their grandmothers knew who couldn't read—that's a fact.'

'I'm afraid that is what is the matter everywhere—that, or something like it. Try England. What are the popular tunes and ballads now? I mean among the real people—the people who once circulated and preserved the old fairy-tales and the old

songs, known now only to philologists, anti-
quaries, and musical historians?   Music-hall
songs ! " Chevy Chase " and " Greensleeves "
must make way for " Hi-tiddly-hi-ti !" and
" Ask a Pleeceman !"   Isn't that so, Dick ?'
  ' Indeed it is ! I haven't lived in London
among them without finding that out.'
  ' The class most usually described as the
People seem to me to have set their maiden
fancies wallowing in the trough of Zolaism,
varnished over with artificial sentimentality,
and a kind of stupid humour made up of
repeated catchwords and a coarse cynicism,
which consists of attributing everything to
the lowest possible motives, and, judging
from the enthusiastic reception given it,
not altogether an unjust estimate of the
average character.   A recognises the appli-
cability of the allusions to B, and *vice-versâ*,
and they both applaud.   What do they
read ?   The men read odds, the women
novelettes, the boys crime-heroism, and all
three the crimes, divorces, and accidents,
the more revolting and prurient the details

the better. If this is a libel, why do the newspapers, which depend on the People for their circulation, make a speciality of such subjects ?'

' It's the wrong sort of education they're after getting, and there's too many of them ; they lead hard lives enough, Lord help them : and they want excitement, and are not particular as to the kind.'

' Yes ; it will take us a generation or two more of blundering to find out that the first thing to teach people is how to lead happy lives, or, failing that, how best to bear unhappy ones. And by that time we shall all be a monotonous mob of millions all exactly alike, with no taste, no individual or parental responsibility, no perception of beauty, or freedom, or wrong, or right, all living in " dwellings," all belonging to one huge trades union, housed and fed and taught our highest ideas by the Social Democratic Federation, and ruled despotically by a Vigilance Committee of total abstainers. The prisons will be opened and turned into dwellings for such of the un-employed as do not happen to be in them already, and the contents of the National Gallery and British Museum will be sold to foreigners to make room for the Salvation Army, endowed by tithes from everybody's wages, and given authority to morally " picket " us all, and be literary censor.'

' Now let's talk of something else,' said Nora, ' and forget all about London. We came here to get rid of it.'

' You are right ; we won't let it haunt and follow us. I'll tell you a song a great German poet made, of which I was reminded when I was telling you of the poor lost elfin king, and the dark fate on his family. You must excuse the wording of it, because it is difficult to translate so as to give the force and form in another language. I must tell you that the Ilse is a river, supposed to be speaking to the poet while wandering in the Hartz Mountains.

'I am the Princess Ilse,
    And dwell in the Ilsenstein:
Come with me to my castle,
    Be happy and be mine.

'Thy weary head I'll moisten
    With water from my spring.
Thou shalt forget thy sorrows,
    Thou sorrow-stricken thing.

'White are my arms and bosom,
    And in them thou shalt lie
And rest, and hear in dreamland
    Old tales of times gone by.

'And I will soothe and give thee
    The kisses I once gave
To our good Emperor Henry,
    Who lies now in his grave.

'The dead are dead and buried,
    The living only live:
And I am alive and passing fair,
    With a laughing heart to give.

'Come down into my castle,
    Down to my crystal halls,
Where ladies and knights are dancing,
    And feasting are squires and thralls.

'Come where the silk trains rustle,
    And steel spurs clang as they go
Amid the music of fiddles,
    And trumpets the small dwarfs blow.

'My white arms I'll wind round thee
    As once I wound them round
The Emperor Henry, and deafened his ears
    From hearing the trumpet sound.'

After a little silence, Nora said :

'I like that.'

Then Cunningham said :

'So do I. I wish you could have the original instead. There, I suppose we had better go to our hotel and dreamland now, or the moonlight will go to our heads. Get up any time you like to-morrow ; there are no trains to catch. I'm afraid I've given you rather a dismal evening.'

'It has been beautiful, and you know it has. Dick, you are not to sit up late and keep Mr. Cunningham up ; he has all the trouble of looking after us like children, and I expect he's fit to be tired.'

'I am accustomed to late hours,' replied Cunningham. 'I think Dick and I will just get into a proper yawnful state over a glass or two of *Franziskaner-bräu* and a pipe, and then retire.'

* * * * *

Next morning, Dick happening to be alone with Nora for a little while, she said :

'He's different when you know him, isn't he ?'

'He is, and he takes a lot of knowing, too.   I think we don't know all of him yet.'

'It is difficult to make him talk about himself.'

'But there would be a story or two if he did, I fancy.   Any way, he's a fine man, and a good comrade.'

CHAPTER XXIII.

On Monday morning they left the bright streets and ornate stately squares, the great palaces of painting and sculpture, the long green *Englischer Garten*, the Isar rushing gray in the sunlight, white in the moonlight, the tall lieutenants and *Rittmeister* in turquoise blue or dark green frocks, and the many various rival *Braüe* of the Bavarian capital behind them, and began to thread valleys and gorges between fir-clad hills, where the little houses began to assume an Alpine appearance, with low obtuse-angled roofs, weighted with stones, far-projecting eaves, and sometimes fretted wooden balconies.

Dick and Cunningham leaned back in

their seats, with German cigars in *Weichsel* holders drooping languidly from the corners of their mouths, and were immensely comfortable and serenely placid. Nora sat in an opposite corner to them, watching everything eagerly from the window. It was another fine warm day, and they had passed the fields by this time, where the crucifixes stood at every cross-road and by-way, where the tillers of the soil were enjoying a good deal of rest. The Bavarian peasant seems to sleep out of doors a good deal, and takes life very pleasantly.

'All this,' Dick said, 'ought to attract Nora's sympathy, to see so much godliness and laziness mixed up together. Oh, they are a fine people, these Bavarians. I love them.'

'You're just as lazy as I am,' said Nora, unmoved.

'I'm lazy. Thou art lazy. He is lazy. Be ye lazy. Let us be lazy,' said Cunningham through his teeth, without moving his cigar or changing his position.

'Now, where are we going to?' said Dick. 'I forgot to ask you that when we started.'

'We are going through the Tirol. We halt to-day at Innsbruck, the chief town of it, rather pretty, and our last stopping-place before Italy. To-morrow we shall cross the Alps. To-morrow night we may hope to be in Verona, where Romeo and Juliet played about lang syne.' The orphans expressed proper rapture, and Cunningham added : 'I should tell you that we shall pass out of Germany into Austria in an hour or so.'

'Will we indeed?' said Dick. 'Customs again, then, I suppose?'

'Yes. At Kufstein you will undergo the *Königlich Kaiserlich Katholisch und Apostolisch Steuer - Revision.* You will observe yellow and black to predominate instead of sky-blue and white on turnpike-poles and post-boys, and an eagle with two heads instead of a lion and chequers, or a one-headed eagle, will be the indigenous fowl.'

' Do they talk German ?'

' Yes.   Only it gets into rather a different brogue, and they are, if possible, more polite than the Bavarians.'

' Look here, we had different colouring, as you're saying, and different postage-stamps, and another head on the gold money, in Bavaria : why didn't we have a Custom-house ?   I know I ought to know, but I don't, and you said travelling ought to be an education, so you might lecture on these points for a minute or two.'

' Bavaria is a kingdom in itself, but is part of the German Empire, and the same Customs arrangements apply there as in most other parts of the empire.   Bavaria may be said to have a qualified sort of Home Rule.'

' More power.   I thought there was some sort of good angel looking after Bavaria.   But the Emperor's got a big berth, if a kingdom like Bavaria's one of his front-gardens, so to speak.'

' The   German   Emperor   is   King   of

Prussia, and lord over three kings and countless princes, grand-dukes, and leader of an army of a million and a half at least.'

' And a fine army it is, too ! I've watched them every time I had a chance. I've had my eye on them. I've never seen the French, but if they've got anything to beat this lot I'd like to see it. Little, strong, healthy, bow-legged men with bright eyes, brown faces, and dusty clothes these are, and great strapping officers and drilled like —like a steam engine. They mean business.'

' The officers in Munich were very fine men,' said Nora.

' Now about Austria ?' pursued Dick ; 'if you would give this infant school a few leading tips about that country, it would improve our minds.'

' Don't improve his mind too much,' said Nora, ' or he will suffer from over-pressure.'

' Come nearer,' said Dick ; ' I can't reach to kick you.'

' They don't grow kings so freely as in

Germany—or, rather, they do ; but they are all united in one person. The Emperor of Austria is the successor, strictly speaking, of the old Emperors of Rome.'

' Julius Caysar and that lot ?'

' Yes. Only, as a matter of fact, I don't think Julius Cæsar ever was Emperor. Well, the Emperor is one of a celebrated and historic family, and when he is in Hungary he is King ; also, I believe, in Bohemia. In Hungary they speak a different language, and have their own postage-stamps and legislative assemblies— Home Rule, in fact. The great thing in these Home-Ruled fragments of big empires seems to me to have your own pattern of postage-stamps and post-cards. The army is common to the whole empire, as, of course, it must be if any sort of *Zusammen-Hang*, as they call it here, is to be kept up at all. The money consists of florins, or gulden, and kreuzers. You will find it a delightful puzzle, now you are used to one decimal coinage, to get used to another of different value, and by the time you have mastered it partially, the Italian currency will come in and upset both. I may tell you that a gulden is worth a hundred kreuzers, and that a kreuzer is worth nothing particular, but is accepted by beggars. A gulden usually occurs in the form of a greenish-gray oblong piece of paper with " Ein Gülden " on one side and " Egy Forint " on the other ; kreuzers usually four or ten at a time in thick wads of copper, or thin laminæ of a pinkish-white pewtery stuff. There is a big army. You will be able to form your own opinion on it from observation. The characteristic point about Austria is the number of different races and languages existing together under one crown—Poles, Magyars, Germans, Czechs, Italians, Slavs, and more I don't remember.'

'They understand over here,' said Dick, 'how to work all these different factions together. Put them all in the same uniform and drill them, that's the trick of it.'

Cunningham laughed :

' That is one way of putting it, certainly ;
and a good deal of truth in it, too. You
will be pleased to hear that a " snack " will
be obtainable at Kufstein, probably taking
the form of a solid *table d'hôte.*'

' I'll be there.'

And in a short time they were all there,
after enjoying the excitement of watching
for the exact point where Bavaria ceased
and Austria began, and having a *pro-forma*
examination of luggage at the hands of the
dark, polite, grave, languid little men who
represented the *K. K. Steuer-Amt* in those
odd high black *képis* so all-pervading in
Official and Military Austria, and they
enjoyed the mid-day meal awaiting them at
the station, and struggled for the first time
with the problem of expressing marks and
pfennigs in terms of guldens and kreuzers.

Later in the afternoon they came into
the bright white town of Innsbruck, standing in the middle of a wide and sunny plain,
surrounded by an amphitheatre of far-off
snow-peaked mountains, and they roamed

among the tall streets and old houses, so
different in style to those of the other towns
they had visited, marvelled at the priests, or
other ecclesiastics in white or black drapery,
or both, surmounted by prosaic *fin-de-siècle*
bowler hats, admired the little blue-gray
Tirolese riflemen, and occasional officers in
short tight-fitting tunics of electric-blue, or
black with narrow yellow piping, four ornate
pocket-flaps, drab pantaloons, and the inevitable high *képi*, like nothing else worn anywhere in the world, and expressed qualified
approval of the Tirolese country-women in
wide shallow stiff black hats, and unqualified
approval of the stalwart ' mountainy ' men
in breeches and leggings and feathered hats.

They also had an opportunity of experiencing that wind which blows the dust
in every direction, makes you hot and as
dry as the desert, makes your eyes water
and gives you neuralgia all at the same
time ; and they made a rapid escape back
to their unpretending old hotel, where they
had a very cosy supper, and spent most of

the evening indoors, comforted by the mild
warmth of a tall blue crockery stove of
strange device. Dick's supply of cigars and
tobacco having given out, he was introduced
after supper to the K.K.K. and A. variety
indigenous to Austria, and smoked a cigar
with grave expectant curiosity, saying he
had already made his will.

'Now, I want to know exactly where we
have been, and the way we have come, ever
since we started,' said Nora. 'I don't want
to go on further without understanding
clearly where I've been and how I got there,
or everything will get mixed up like a
dream—though it's a very pleasant one.'

'All right.' And Cunningham went upstairs and brought down a map, and spread
it on the table, and sat in front of it with
a blue chalk pencil. 'Now look here.'
Nora stood leaning on the back of his chair,
and looked over his shoulder. 'We will
mark the route lightly with blue, putting
a blue circle round the places we stopped
at.'

'Yes, and we'll go on doing that every time we stop.'

'We will. It's a capital idea.'

And Cunningham thought he would cheerfully map out a route from Jerusalem to Madagascar *viâ* Peru if this girl would lean over him in this way and criticise all the time. Only the provoking part was that she did it with such matter-of-fact coolness and absence of self-consciousness that he felt he might as well have been a mere brother. 'Well, here's London, where horrible voices are at this moment shouting, "Liverpool Street! Penny all the way!" And here's Queenborough, where you took ship. There's where you crossed the sea.' Blue rigid line to Flushing.

'What, only that little way to take all night?'

'That little way is some miles if you reckon by the scale. Then we crossed Holland along this line, Breda, Boxtel, etc., and so into Germany—Kempen, Krefeld, Neuss, Köln. There we make the first blue circle.'

And so he went on, concluding : ' And here we are now, sampling Tirol wine and the Imperial Royal Catholic Apostolic Tobacco-Monopoly.'

' Don't talk like that !'

' My good lady, it is not I ; it is on the labels, so to speak.   It's the correct official term, to the best of my belief, and quite serious.   " Gott erhalte Franz den Kaiser !" '

Dick chuckled.

Nora said : ' Let me look at the map a little more.'

' As long as you like.'

And she followed the route marked slowly with the finger of her right hand, while her left arm rested on the back of Cunningham's chair, and the fragrance of her black hair bewildered him so that he sat motionless like an enchanted man.   Then she stood up again, and moved away, saying :

' Thank you.   I've learned a lot of geography this evening.   Look, Dick.'

Cunningham reversed the map, pushed it

across the table to Dick, who studied it intelligently, from a tactical standpoint, and got up himself and poured out and drank a glass of the red draught wine. They had the little *Gast-Stube* to themselves that evening.

'I hope,' said Cunningham, 'you won't think me an awful prig lecturing like this, but you asked for it, you know.'

'Of course,' said Dick, 'it's us that ought to apologize for boring you to explain things to us in words of one syllable. But I think the class is getting on, and doing you credit.'

'Yes,' Nora said. 'It's very kind of you. Please, teacher, how long does it take for letters to get to England?'

'About three, or perhaps four, days. Better tell them to answer to Post Restante, Venice.'

'Venice? Think of our going there. I think we really ought to write to somebody. We haven't told a single soul where we are, or written a line since we started.'

'Some of us ought,' said Dick.

'I suppose that means you won't be at the trouble?'

'That's what it means, my dear.' replied Dick, serenely pulling at his six-kreuzer cigar.

'I'll get the waiter to give you paper and stamps,' said Cunningham, 'if you want it. Will it be an extensive correspondence?'

'Oh no ; I'll sacrifice myself for you all, and write one letter to Jane Smalley, and you can send messages.'

'That's a capital idea. Describe yourself as sitting with two benevolent but exhausted men who are unequal to the exertion of writing, but beg that their sins may be remembered in that nymph's orisons,' said Cunningham, going to obtain stationery and a very pretty stamp.

CHAPTER XXIV.

A LITTLE time passed, during which the treasures and curiosities of Schloss Ambras, and the stately halls of the imperial residence, were duly exhibited by polite liveried menials to our travellers, and explained in the mixture of pomp and statistics composing the phraseology usual in such functions. They also saw the formidable-looking group of iron kings guarding Maximilian's grave in the Franciscan church, and after a few more walks among the white or yellow lofty houses, with their strange old frescoed fronts, they bought photographs, paid bills, and were soon being dragged slowly by a panting train up among the dark fir-trees, rushing streams, and snow-streaked slopes and peaks which surround the way to Brenner.

Up to the chill summit of the pass and over it they went, and down the other side, where the streams began to flow in an opposite direction, running with them now, down the Valley of the Eisach, past the imposing stone fortress of Franzensfeste, guarding the south-western gate of Austria, past Brixen, and Botzen, where the darkness hid everything, and so through the great fertile Botzen valley and plain, invisible save for a distant light or two, for the night had now come, and the changed scenery could not be seen with the eyes, and Trent and Roveredo were mere names, lamps, and platforms.

But there was the strange, mysterious feeling of being in a new climate—of being on the warm side of the great Alpine watershed, where a new, rich vegetation scented a balmier air, different from the bracing terebinthine atmosphere behind on the other slope of Brenner, warmer, more languorous, and yet more exciting, where the fire-flies were restlessly darting about the banks outside the train windows like little meteors, and a certain beautiful Irish girl was watching them with admiration and ' strange wonder in her eyes.'

' It's got powerful warm,' observed Dick, knocking the ashes out of his pipe on the window-sill.

' Yes. This pass is arranged like the stages of a Turkish bath taken backwards. You begin with the temperate mildness of Innsbruck (when a Föhn isn't blowing), go on to the icy chilliness of the higher pass, where you huddle overcoats on and expect snow, then you switchback down the other slope, the fir-trees turn into mulberries, " out flounce " vineyards, and you want both windows open and the roof off.'

' I say, we'll have to wear flannels or something to-morrow.'

' Oh yes, we must put on cooler things to-morrow. Do you know those coloured Oxford shirtings ? I think they're rather dodgy things for a warm place—almost better than flannels ; I've got some with me.'

'No ; I just stick to white flannels. I can wear a tweed coat, and a necktie, and a straw hat with them, you know. I don't want the Italians to take me for a professional cricketer.'

Nora turned her head again towards the inner life of that whirling microcosm, the railway compartment, and said :

'How in the world *can* you two prose about flannel shirts, when we're just coming into Italy, and the fire-flies all dancing in the dark alongside ? I can't see anything but them below and the stars above, and I can't think of anything but Italy. The very air is different, and full of beautiful dreams.'

'You've been dreaming a bit, any way,' said Dick. 'You were sitting in that corner of yours a little while ago with your head on one side and your mouth open.'

'That's a libel, Nora,' said Cunningham calmly.

' I know it. Where are we now ? Not in Italy yet ?'

' Not yet, though it's getting so warm. We are still in the territory of the Emperor of Austria, but not for much longer; we shall get to Ala directly.'

' We have a halt there, I suppose,' said Dick, ramming a fresh pipeload tight with his thumb, 'and fool about with the luggage in the usual way ?'

' Just that.'

' Will there be anything to eat ?'

Cunningham and Nora both laughed, and the former said :

' Probably a little bread and cheese, and cold veal or sausage, and a bottle of red wine. But we shall have supper in Verona, "now the stage of two hours' traffic," to adapt Shakespeare to railway conditions. Let us hope to meet Two Gentlemen.'

' I want to see Juliet's house,' said Nora.

' Yes ; you shall see the House of the Capulets. Have you got a Shakespeare with you?' Cunningham asked, in the matter-of-course tone in which he might have said, ' Have you got a pocket-handker-chief?'

' No.'

' Well, there's one in my bag, so you can read up the play and get into a proper frame of mind first.'

Here the train came to a standstill, and waited for a long time, with whistlings, and the sound of a trumpet, and thick darkness ; heads were thrust out of windows, and ex-citement and impatience grew. Then an impulsive jangling move, another stop, lights, voices, the door flung open, a number of excited persons chattering in a new lan-guage, a big, bare room with the usual wooden-ribbed counter, civil little men in brown-and-yellow nautical-looking caps and neat tunics, rather short in the place where dignity demands length, a *dolce far niente* kind of examination of baggage, a little waiting-room with a table, glasses of red wine standing in thick white saucers, bread,

and long, thin cigars with straws sticking
out of them.

Such was Nora's ' impressionist ' recollec-
tion of Ala.

' Then we're in Italy now?' said she.

'What? Oh yes. We shall be in Verona
soon, where you will, no doubt, be glad to
have supper, Scanlan ?'

'Faith, I will! Here's Italy's health!
Not bad stuff this. I suppose they make
it about here ?'

' I suppose so. Nora, we must continue
that blue chalk line on the map to-morrow,
mustn't we ?'

' We must. It's very important. We've
been through so many pleasant countries
and beautiful places on the way, I don't
know which I like best.'

' Good old Bavaria,' said Dick, ' as far as
I've gone, obtains the macaroon !'

' Don't be vulgar, now,' said Nora in a
superior manner.

*   *   *   *   *

More impressions. The train again. A dusty, sallow - brown, black - moustached, smiling person climbing in and making polite inquiries in Italian.

'Is this a brigand now?' calmly from Dick.

'No; ticket - collector, prosaic and innocuous.'

Loud tenor shoutings of 'P-r-r-onti! P'tenza!'

Further journeying through warm darkness.

A brief stoppage, 'Porta Nuova.' A slow curvilinear advance. Verona. A large, stony, lamp-lit station; little soldiers standing about in brief dark-blue tunics buttoning *en plastron*, with turned-down collars adorned with a star at each corner, red epaulets, and hard round caps; a magnificent gendarme in a cocked hat and plume. An omnibus. Ramparts. *Pro forma* stoppage by the *dazio municipale*. Rumbling and jerking through dark narrow streets of tall prison-like houses, with square barred windows six or seven feet above the ground. The welcome light and shelter of the hotel of the Golden Dove ; bowing servants with fascinating manners.

'The further we go, the politer everybody gets,' observed Dick.

A merry supper of savoury omelette and red wine, and then sound sleep.

Next morning Cunningham came downstairs about nine, and, finding nobody of his party, went and stood in the arched entrance looking at the street, the passers-by, and the diagonal patches of bright sunlight on the houses. The air was alive with the melodious shoutings of those who had something to sell, and the cracking of whips and jingling of bells of those who drove waggons ; and every conceivable method of making a good rattle, jingle, yell, hoot, or bellow was being employed with or without the slightest possible pretext.

Two men, at a little distance from the door, who were supposed to be mending the pavement, were lying in the middle of the

street at full length, with brilliant sunshine
on their curly black heads and mellow
tanned faces, talking loudly and rapidly, and
playing a kind of infantine game with the
stones forming their stock-in-trade.   Little
bersaglieri in broad hats and drooping cocks'
feathers passed by every few minutes, with
an air of half-unconscious picturesqueness,
falling by natural genius into the attitudes
and expressions proper to wearers of such
hats.   Sometimes an officer, in a little
pulpy cap, brilliant silver epaulets, the
unfortunate tunic, which is *vir formosus
superne*, but below the waist atrophies pre-
maturely into a little tail with paltry pleats
and gathers, and gray pantaloons with a
red or black stripe, which are well enough.

Soon Nora arrived, looking cool and fresh
in a dress of lemon-coloured nun's veiling ;
and she also came to the door and looked
out.

'Good-morning.   Did you sleep well ?'

'I did ; very well, thank you.   Hasn't
Dick come in yet ?'

' Come in ?   I didn't know he was out.'

' Indeed he is !   He got up an hour ago, and said he would go for a walk.   He didn't like to wake you ; he said you were sleeping so well.'

' Enterprising.   Likewise considerate.   I suppose he proceeded to lose himself, as a preliminary ?   However, Verona is not large, and he can always take a cab, and mention the name of the hotel.'

' He took your guide-book and map out of your room when you were sleeping.'

' I undervalued his military training and instincts.   A trustworthy intuition tells me he will soon feel hungry, and that that will bring him back.   It's a funny place, isn't it ?'

' It's very wonderful !   I'm longing to go out and see it all.   What an awful row they make !'

' Yes ; they like a good healthy noise. It seems busy and industrious and all that sort of thing—which is just what they are not, bless them !   Look at those two on the

pavement there.   I wonder how many hours
a day they are paid to do that kind of thing,
and how long it takes to lay a yard of pavement or tramline here.'

'I like that.   I expect to be quite at
home here.   You don't know how lazy I
can be.'

'I have some idea.   But I sympathize.
I never want to do any work again.   Lotus-
land for ever !'

And Cunningham thought of his lonely old
chambers ; of swarming, pushing, struggling,
fog-laden Fleet Street ; of sporting tele-
grams, of City buses, of falling flakes of
soot ; and then he looked at this lovely girl,
at her curling black hair, eyes like violets
in solution, her skin, to which the sun had
given a little golden-brown tinge, and at
her whole kindly, impulsive, honest self,
standing beside him in the grace and glory
of her strength and symmetry ; and a dream
came into his head of journeying always in
lazy, old-world, sun-burnt cities, through
fragrant fir-clad forests, beside great historic

rivers, in the sight of far-off snow-peaked mountains, with her always near him—of losing her never — while summer blazed, while winter whitened, till the time when two more must cross the cold dark river.

Nora produced, after some searching for a pocket in the new summer frock, a penny, and silently proffered it to Cunningham, who looked at it, then at her, and replied :

' I catch on. But they are worth much more than that.'

' I dare say. But you looked so very—I don't know quite what to call it—thoughtful, I wanted to know.'

' Did I ?'

' You did. You looked as if you were thinking of somebody or something you had lost long ago.'

' It wasn't quite that. Yet I did lose somebody long ago.'

' There is a story about that, I think—a story you never tell to anyone.'

' You can call it a story, I suppose. And I never have told it to anyone—yet.'

'I don't like to ask, but I should like you to tell it to me.'

'Perhaps Verona is the place of all others to tell it in, where so much love and sorrow once were buried. There, it all happened a long time ago, you know. I was once staying for awhile at Dresden on the Elbe, the capital of Saxony, you know, a great place for pictures and painting, among other things. It was during a Long when I was at Trinity. And there was a girl, an English girl. It doesn't matter what she was like, but I thought her beautiful. She studied painting, and lived with her mother and sister. They were pleasant enough people, poor gentlefolks who wandered about the world. This girl of mine, who never was mine, was rather delicate, and was capricious and flippant, in a kindly way, and loved fun above all things, and sometimes would mildly shock her mother by the things she said, but was in reality as unselfish and pure-minded as—as anyone ever was. But she was original and witty,

and if a thing was funny, she saw it was
funny, profane and unconventional even
though it might seem to say so. Well, I
was too young to really understand some
things, perhaps, and I never understood
that that girl really was good enough to—
to love a rather ordinary youth such as I
was. No one had ever done it before, and
no one has since, as far as I know. But I
have since come to think that she did, and
that, if I had only known it, or had the
audacity to speak of such things to her, I
might have had the answer I wished for,
and things might have turned out differently.
And so we went on, talking and amusing
each other, and I loving her as one loves the
impossible, unattainable thing, and listening
to her, and remembering always every word
she said, and proud when I could make her
laugh by some undergraduate story or
youthful witticism of mine, as we sat in
summer evenings, all four of us, in the
gardens by the river listening to music,
while the sunset reddened over the Elbe

bridges. And then autumn came, I went back to Trinity, and they went away here, to Italy, because she was delicate. And here in Italy she lies buried. I haven't told the story well, because I am not used to telling it at all, and it isn't much of a story for anybody but me—and, as I tell you, it all happened a long time ago.'

' Thank you for telling me. I knew there was a story.'

' How ?'

' I don't know. I knew there was one. And you never told it to anyone at all except me ?'

' Never.'

' And I will never tell it to anyone. You meant that too, though you didn't say so ?'

' Yes ; I imagined you would understand that.'

' Then, I do. Here comes Dick.'

And a tall figure in flannel trousers, a dark-blue neck-handkerchief, a brown tweed jacket and a straw hat appeared, bearing a red Baedeker's ' Northern Italy.' He took off his hat and wiped his sun-tanned face, and laughed.

' Well, I'm ready for my breakfast. They woke me up early with the divil's own delights they're kicking up outside, so I thought I'd get up and go and have a look round. It's a fine old town, but I'm after thinking it's seen better days.'

' Most towns in Italy have. Have a magnificent career behind them, as Heine said of Alfred de Musset, " Ein junger Mensch mit einer sehr schöner Vergangenheit vor sich." Picturesque people, aren't they ?'

' Oh, they're lovely people !'

' Come and sit down ; here's a table. I must break to you, Scanlan, that it is customary here to have only some coffee and bread-and-butter now, for if you take more you will spoil your appetite for the real business breakfast, which comes off between eleven and twelve, and is generally good. There's a place down alongside the river where we can have that out of doors, when we are tired of walking about.'

' Oh yes, I saw the river. There's a queer old bridge over it, with a red-brick castle at one end. There was a cat in the river— been there some time, too, I should say. I supposed it was the original " poor cat in the Adige " Shakespeare talks of.'

' I think a man who deliberately invents a revolting anecdote for the purpose of leading up to that crowning atrocity—at break-fast-time, too—deserves to have to calculate the worth of all our remaining gulden and kreuzers in terms of lire and centesimi at the exchange of the day.'

' Ah, he was a fine man, Shakespeare ! Don't abuse him. What are we to do this morning ?'

' Go and change our money. Then walk about and look at Verona. And for pity's sake leave that red Baedeker behind ! I'll tell you what the places are.'

' Yes, it does attract notice. Several jokers began conversing with me, and wanted

me to do something or other. Guides, I
imagined. I tried talking Irish at first, but
I learned with a little practice the best thing
was to point to my ears and mouth, gurgle
sinfully, and shake my head. Another time
I'll bark like a dog and snap.'

'You'll do that when you're alone by
yourself then,' said Nora.

'In any case,' observed Cunningham
(well knowing that the imaginative but kind-
hearted Grenadier had really done nothing of
the sort, but probably given gratuities far
beyond their expectations or deserts to
the plausible professional beggars), 'you
would be surrounded by the available gen-
darmerie, and immured in a dungeon somewhere below the level of the Adige—probably in that red Castello Vecchio.'

'Ah, well, these adventures all come in
the day's work. It's fine and warm here, I
will say.'

'Yes,' said Nora; 'I thought I would put
on a summer dress.'

'Mighty fine ye look, too !'

Cunningham only said :

'I think you will find that you were quite right.'

And then they went out, along the shady narrow streets, into the blazing glare of the Piazza Vittorio Emanuele, where is an effigy of that popular and virile but marvellous ill-favoured hero, and explored Diocletian's amphitheatre, where Dick said :

'Now you begin to feel how old this country really is. Those ancient Romans were building these things and had been civilizing the world for centuries when you English and Scotch were just savages, with nobody except the grand old kings of Ireland to show you what civilization meant.'

' Did they ?' said Cunningham mildly.

'Indeed and indeed. And sent over the good missionaries who made you Christians centuries B.C.'

' Yes, to be sure. I forgot.'

' Is this where the martyrs of the Church used to meet the wild beasts ?' asked Nora.

' Most likely. Seems strange to us who stand here now, doesn't it ?'

' It does. And to think they saw that blue sky we see, and felt this same hot sun we feel, so many centuries ago, all those poor people—men like you and girls like me, maybe.'

' Down below I'll show you the cells they kept them and the beasts in, and how they came out into the arena.'

'I don't think I would like to see them. And did people sit round on these stones and look on for amusement—ladies, and maybe little children, and all ?'

' On these very stones.'

Nora, who was sitting down for a moment, hastily rose, and said :

' Let us go away now. There are ghosts in this place.'

And they went, and Cunningham led them to a long narrow crowded street leading towards a sunny, more crowded, chattering, parti-coloured market-place, and in that Via Capello he pointed out an old house with a crumbling stone-arched entrance, high above it shuttered windows, and right at the top a stone balcony under the flat projecting roof. Cunningham said :

'The house is, of course, like all these houses, built on the courtyard system, and not intended to be appreciated from the street. *The* balcony and garden, if any, would be at the back. That is the House of the Capulets. Tradition assigns it, and I fancy tradition is right.'

'There! I am glad I have seen that. Such a sorrowful thing, too ! Verona seems full of sad things. But there is something beautiful about some sad things,' she added, looking at Cunningham, 'isn't there ? And this is one. Can I get a photograph of this ?'

'Certainly, and the amphitheatre too, if you like.'

'No, that is dreadful. I shall dream about that. I want to forget it.'

As they walked on, she said :

'I was awake early, too. I made Dick get me your Shakespeare, when he went to steal your Baedeker. And I read the play.'

'I'm glad of that. It happened a long time ago, too,' he added with a little smile at her.

Then they saw the old Piazza de Signori, with its white awnings sheltering gabbling marketers, its great municipal tower, the building and statues, the monuments of the Scaligers, and all that was of interest and beauty in that oasis of a bygone world, rich in romance, beauty and bloodshed. Cunningham pointed out to Dick how an ancient Roman house had a mediæval Italian house grafted on it, and dovetailed into it, combining as the two histories, the two civilizations, pre- and post-Christian, in Italy only do combine.

Then Dick suggested, 'That breakfast you were talking of is almost due.' And they sat at a table in the pleasant riverside *Trattoria Cola*, and were very glad of the rest, refreshment, and shade. After the *collazione* they went home to rest in their respective rooms. Dick, after wrestling unsuccessfully with a 'long Virginia,' and spending four matches over it, filled the faithful *dhudeen* with the remains, and was soon sound asleep, with ashes on his chest.

Cunningham, whose tobacco had also given out, got through the majority of his Cavour, and reflected : ' Tobacco is not an Italian strong point. Thus far protection and monopoly don't come off. But it's getting very evident that if I'm alone with this girl much oftener I shall say something. And that will spoil the whole trip, perhaps. But if it didn't ! If it improved the whole trip unspeakably ! There, I must try and let it alone. Things are very nice as they are, and it would be stupid to precipitate a horrible collapse—which would make the world a fraud, and the sunshine a mockery, and my life a very empty thing, made up of sad memories and foiled hopes. Well, I'm happy now. I must let it all drift, and hope for the best. She is the only one— since

' " Und du bist todt, mein todtes Kind."

And you do not know now anything at all. You do not know that I have gone sorrowing through the world for ten years since I lost you. You never even knew I loved you, then, to-day, and always, as the student did the poor *Wirthin's Töchterlein*. But if you do know anything at all, where you are, you will forgive me for loving the girl who was sorry for you and for me. For I do love her, or I would not have told her that story.'

And then peace came on his eyelids, and a dream. He dreamed he was on the old bridge by the Castello Vecchio—and yet the passers-by were talking in German, and far away among the tall old trees stood a stately building which was sometimes the Hof-Kirche and Opera-house, and sometimes the New Court of John's. And there stood beside him a girl, who had been dead, but seemed to be alive, who put her arms round him, and said:

'I am not dead, and I shall never die, and I have always kept the violets you gave me, and they have never died, and will never die. Here they are in my old white dress I wore on summer Sundays by the Elbe.'

'But they told me you were dead. I wore black for you round my heart.'

'I am alive. Look at me.' And for a moment he saw the face which one scarcely ever sees really in dreams, and it had become the face of Nora. 'Who am I? You know me. I was and I am. I said to Romeo, "My bounty is as boundless as the sea, my love as deep." I wore your violets when I died in Rome. I am Love.'

He replied with that stupidity only possible in dreams :

'But Love is a little boy, allegorically.'

And no answer came, and there was nothing at all but broad water and gray mist, with scattered violets floating on the water.

＊　　　＊　　　＊　　　＊　　　＊

'That's queer too. I am afeard

> '"All this is but a dream
> Too flattering sweet to be substantial."

I wonder, now, what Nora has been dreaming about. I've a good mind to ask her by-and-by.' When he did so, as they began another stroll later in the afternoon, she replied with some little embarrassment :

'Oh, a lot of nonsense ! I can't remember.'

And Cunningham had to be satisfied with that.

CHAPTER XXV.

In the course of time Cunningham and the orphans got as far as Venice, and dwelt in a pleasant, unpretentious *albergo* with windows giving on the Piazza of St. Mark, where they did not suffer from English influence, directly or indirectly. That is to say, the prices were not doubled for everything, the guests did not ignore each other's presence, look suspicious of the dishes, or embarrassed if a stranger offered them the salad, or converse in guarded whispers, or sit in blank silence, and the wine was not treated as an extra. I could write a long and instructive excursus on the English influence in foreign lands, on the comfort and blessing they are, both in civilized and

in savage countries ; how glad one ought to
be, and always is, to find their lawn-tennis,
their church, their brandy-and-soda, their
races and their afternoon tea in the one,
and their crude whisky and missionary
bishops in the other, and their delightful
ignoring of the existence and feelings of the
' natives ' in both, except as persons to do
work for them or provide them with amusement or profit.   I could tell stories of
Englishmen who sent their guides in to tell
a Norwegian land and water proprietor that
they ' wanted ' his river to fish, and when
he in all sincere hospitality placed it at
their disposal, treated him, and the food he
offered them, as subjects for that delightful
and refined form of jocularity called ' chaff,'
and laughed because he did not understand
why they laughed.   Norwegians with rivers
know better now.   I have seen an Englishman, one who might be called ' an awfully
decent sort,' who never put on ' side,' or
missed church (in a tall hat) on Sundays,
and knew something of ' smashing volleys '

and having a ' beastly head on,' sit, in spite
of all these advantages and experiences, at a
gathering of polite and ceremonious German
Ein-jährigers, doctors, and candidates, at
which he was an invited guest, with a brown
' bowler ' on the back of his head, never
taking the trouble to observe that such a
decoration was at all exceptional, quite
satisfied with himself, whispering to his
English-speaking friend, and laughing at
the attempts of his hosts to speak English.
I have heard English ladies (dressed as
English ladies abroad alone dare to dress),
in a railway train, making loud personal
remarks about their fellow-travellers, imagining that since the latter spoke their own
un-English language, they could not possibly
understand any other. When one of those
fellow-travellers took out an old *Standard*
and proceeded ostentatiously to read it, they
had the grace to look ashamed. It was not
intentionally unkind of them, it was only
stupid. And yet they wonder, or do not
believe, when they hear that the English

are unpopular, or thought ridiculous, in other countries.

Well, our friends naturally visited most of the places and things which help to make Venice the unique archipelago of beauty and interest it is, such as the Duomo, the Ducal Palace, the churches, the pictures, the Rialto, the Ghetto, and the wonderful town itself. They looked at the shops in the colonnade of the Piazza, and learned in time that it was impossible to do so without being immediately accosted by pertinacious, plausible young men of Semitic aspect with, 'Good-morning, sare. You vill valk opstars?' which must repel much possible commerce, one would think. They roamed about in gondolas, to the immense satisfaction of Nora in particular, who found it laziness idealized. They went over to Lido, where they enjoyed sea-bathing, followed by a *colazione* on the pier, and they sat in the evenings on the Piazza listening to the band, with ices or *Birra di Monaco*, on which occasions the elegant but

somewhat forward flower-women made a
dead set at Dick, whom, indeed, they insisted on decorating with blossoms at all
hours of the day, as if he was a kind of
shrine.

One afternoon, after a short siesta,
following on a long and tiring morning,
during which they had all been up and,
what is worse, down the very nerve-trying
set of inclined planes of the Campanile of
San Giorgio Maggiore, and subsequently
done some shopping in the Via Ventidue
Marzo, and breakfasted at the Vapore,
Cunningham got up, and not wishing to
disturb the others, who were probably
asleep, strolled out by himself, with the
view of penetrating the obscure labyrinth
of little lanes which lead ' alla Posta,' as
the inscription on the walls indicated, and
inquiring for letters. Having reached the
post and found nothing, he turned back
again, and in the narrow, crowded Merceria,
echoing with the cries of the man who sold
ice-water, saw a tall black figure with

square shoulders and a slender waist, walking towards him with the slow, serene
dignity which characterized the one woman
in the world for him. It was, in short,
Nora, who, tired of resting, had put on a
black grenadine dress and gone on a voyage
of discovery by herself, imagining that her
two fellow-travellers were asleep. She did
not at first see Cunningham, as she was
examining shop-windows full of filigree
gondolas and inlaid duomos, and a perpetual
stream of passers-by intervened—of women
in umber yellow, dark-red, or dull-green
shawls, and clattering slippers, *bersaglieri* in
drooping cocks' feathers, and miscellaneous
chattering, laughing loungers, and he watched
her for a few moments with grave admiration. Very soon, however, she perceived
him, and he thought she looked pleased.

'Hullo!' he said. 'And where are you
going?'

'I don't know,'

'Very well; so am I. Let us go there
together. Where is your brother?'

'Asleep.   I came out by myself.'

'I see.   Where would you like to go?'

'Well, I would really like—if it won't be too long—to go in a gondola.   But just as you please.'

'Oh, I please, of course.   To anywhere particular?'

'Oh no.   Just to go in it.   I was making up my mind when I saw you, whether I had the cheek to do it alone, and what I would say to the man.   But I'm glad you've come. Where have you been?'

'To the post.   There are no letters.'

'Jane ought to write soon.'

'I dare say she has written by this time, but the letters take a long time to come and go.'

They walked out of the narrow, shady Merceria, across the blazing Piazza pavement, accompanied by a mob of pigeons, who seemed to detect a stranger as readily and eagerly as the unabashed Duomo guides, who all assert they are the sacristan.

'I wish I had something for them.'

'They are over-fed, fastidious beasts—
like sturdy beggars. But some time you
shall give them a tribute of biscuits,
and they will all come and pitch on your
shoulders and arms and head. It is very
picturesque. Look at those men and
women going to sleep on the steps in the
shade of the Duomo.'

'I like those shawls they put over
their heads; they are always such pretty
colours. It is a wonderful place entirely—
Venice.'

'Best sermon in stones you could wish
for. Look at that slumbering heap of
gondoliers. Hi! *Poppe!*'

Instantly a swarthy pirate, who knew
them by previous experience, separated himself from the reposing swarm of the Piazzetta,
greeted them with much grace and dignity,
and guided them on board of his gondola,
which had not got the hearse part on, only
a pink-and-white-striped awning. Cunningham handed Nora into her seat and sat
down beside her, and they started slowly

and smoothly off in the direction of the iron bridge, the *Poppe* occasionally muttering spells to himself when anything got in the way, and benevolently refraining from naming to his passengers all the palaces they passed.

'Oh, this is nice, isn't it?' said Nora, leaning back on the black leather-cushioned seat, crossing her feet on the floor at full extent. 'But we mustn't be late, on account of Dick.'

'We shall not be long—not half long enough. We are simply going to our hotel by water; we shall go in at the back-way, as we did coming from the station, only we have to get through a good deal of Canal Grande first, and then turn into one of those narrow curly dead-cat canals, where the Smell lives.'

After a few minutes of pleasant silence, while the gondola floated on with strong, slow impulses up the silent street of palaces, Cunningham said :

'I hope you are enjoying this tour of

ours ?   I think you do, don't you ?   I mean
the whole business.'

' Oh, I can't tell you how much !   I can't
put all I think about it into words ; but I
feel so ignorant among it all.   When we
go looking at pictures of people who lived
in history, or had a great deal to do with
these lovely places, or at old books in
beautiful bindings and illuminated pages,
and you seem to exactly know what it is
all about, and who did it, and when—and
then you know all about the great painters
who died long ago, and the difference between
them, and when they lived, and you can
talk to the people in different countries in
their own language—oh ! it all makes me
feel like a stupid child, who sees that the
sun is large and bright, but doesn't know
what it is for, except, perhaps, to play with,
if someone will get it down.'

' Oh, but don't think like that.   There
is no reason why you should.   You have a
perfectly intelligent appreciation of things,
even if they are new to you, and you grasp

an idea readily enough. It's all a matter
of experience and taste ; you've got the
taste, and you're getting the experience.
Lots of young women in Britain can reel
off " art " names and appropriate adjectives
over afternoon tea, without having a fraction
of your natural appreciation of beautiful
things. And as for languages, you could
learn them just as easily as I, if you
were to try ; and I have no doubt, in the
time to be, you will know lots of them
fluently.'

'I might have been all right if I had
had the same chances when I was young
as other girls. I was not stupid, I don't
think, naturally, but I was idle ; and then
my education was neglected, and we were
very poor, and they couldn't afford to have
me properly taught, except now and then.
And, then, a year or two in a shop doesn't
improve one's mind. You must have been
surprised, I suppose, that I did not drop
my " h's " ?'

'Oh no ! Scotch and Irish people don't

do that, whatever their other faults may be.'

' I wish I wasn't so ignorant.'

Cunningham noticed suddenly that her eyes were just full of tears, and that the slightest cause would precipitate a drop. He said emphatically :

' Oh, nonsense ! You're not at all like your description of yourself. You are not to entertain these depressing fictions.'

She pursued, as if in continuation of her own thoughts, and regardless of his words :

' And that's why I make myself ridiculous sometimes, and lose my temper, and say things I am ashamed of afterwards, as I used to do to you, when I didn't know you properly. I tried to put you right, and only put myself wrong, simply because I was too ignorant to know what a fool I was making of myself; and then I could have burnt my tongue out for doing it, when you calmly explained to me, without seeming to care a bit, in words you would use to a naughty child, what stupid rubbish I was talking.'

'Never mind, we never have rows now, do we?' No reply. 'Do we?' he repeated; then, looking under her hat, which hid part of her face, which was turned away from him, he saw that she was silently crying. The hand nearest him, in a black glove— he had seen her first and oftenest in black gloves—was holding her black lace sunshade, as it lay in her lap, with the point towards her feet. He gently detached that hand, and, holding it in his own, brought it down between them, to a less conspicuous position, where he held it. She did not attempt to move it, but grasped his hand firmly and a little convulsively. He said: 'Don't—don't cry! My—darling!'

She still held his hand fast, and wiped her eyes with the other.

'Gia é!' suddenly bellowed the gondolier raucously, as they shot round a corner into a narrow ditch, where the decaying walls of the houses were a playground for little crabs, and met a barge laden with yellow and green vegetables, which was an occasion for much dexterous navigation and exchange of repartee and malediction.

The two travellers were startled, and sat up in an attitude of exaggerated indifference and propriety, while to Cunningham's eyes, for a moment, all Venice beat like a heart.

Shortly after this they passed the Smell, and then he helped her out of the gondola at the landing, which was close to the back entrance of the restaurant annexed to their hotel. I forget the name of the canal where the Smell lives—I mean the Smell *primus inter pares* (like the Moderator at the General Assembly) ; but if any intending traveller wants to find it, he can write to me, and I will try and describe the way. It is a very rare, very old smell, probably not grown anywhere else. It beats the little back streets near the river at Heidelberg all to nothing, and can afford to smile at the gluey and leathery breezes of Bermondsey ; but having never visited a

Chinese town, I would not like to say that it is utterly without a rival.

Dick was not in the hotel, so the porter said. So Cunningham suggested :

'No use taking the trouble to go upstairs; let's take a turn in the Piazza and look for him. He's sure not to be far off.'

So they went along the colonnade, and the first object that met their eye was Dick, 'colloguing' with the best-looking and forwardest of the flower-women. They did not understand one another's language much, but each had picked up a phrase or two comprehensible to the other, and, as the poet says of the stars,

'Die haben eine Sprache,
Die ist so reich, so schön,
Dass keiner der Philologen,' etc., etc.

Cunningham and Nora watched with great amusement as they approached. Dick had his back to them, but the girl saw them, and, recognising them as belonging to the same party, left Dick abruptly with a pert smile, and pursued her way humming a tune and walking with a good deal of ' side ' on.

Dick turned with a bashful grin to behold his sister, who said :

' *Well !*'

Cunningham observed :

' It's lucky you haven't a more fluent grasp of the language, old man, or you might get landed in a Venetian breach of promise, and get tried before the Duke and the Magnificoes.'

' See, now, you come with me, chummy, and have a drop of nice red Chianti out of a basket ; and Nora, too, if she has been good.'

' Have I been good ?' asked Nora of Cunningham.

' I have no complaint to make,' replied he dryly, adding : ' Have you ?'

She looked at him for a moment out of those soft—often sad—violet eyes, and said :

' No.'

'Come on, then,' said Dick, and they sat at a table at one of the numerous cafés.

'Now, where have you been?' asked Dick.

'I'll begin,' said Cunningham. 'I went out first under the impression that you were all asleep, and went to the post. Finding nothing there, I came back, and in the Merceria, that narrow place, where you go in under the comic clock, you know, I found your sister. Now you can go on,' he said to Nora.

'Then I made Mr. Cunningham get a gondola, and we went to see the Smell.'

'It was at home,' concluded Cunningham. 'But we didn't detain it long, and then landed here and gave the *Poppe* backsheesh. What did you do, Scanlan? But perhaps you would rather relate that when we are alone.'

'Indeed he will relate it now,' said Nora, turning her wineglass round and round, and balancing it to right and left, to the imminent risk of a spill. She was always playing with things, absently, that day.

'I did nothing. When I woke up, which was only half an hour ago——'

'Dormouse,' said Cunningham, 'likewise sloth.'

'Listen, now, while I tell you. I found that you two had gone out, so I went for a little walk on my own hook. I did not get lost very often, and I've made one or two little purchases.'

'I hope you didn't pay the first price they asked,' said Cunningham, 'because there is an air of confiding benevolence about you which means fifty per cent. above the ordinary degree of extortion from a super-subtle Venetian.'

'Oh, I'm not such a fool as I look. I only bought things with the price marked on them. There's a black fan and a little silver gondola, Nora, for you, which is a brooch.'

'You're a good boy, Dick — thanks. They're very pretty indeed, both of them.'

'And here's a meerschaum for you, chummy. I know it is not made here ; but I wanted to give you something useful, and the local products seem to be mostly glass and filigree—pretty enough, to be sure, but not much in a man's line. I've got glass things for Jane Smalley and her mother and sisters ; they're to be packed and sent to the hotel. I haven't made up my mind what to get for Johnny ; I thought you might help me. I was just thinking that over when you met me.'

'Yes,' said Cunningham, 'you looked pensive. And what have you got for yourself ?'

'There, I forgot that entirely !'

'That's you all over, my friend. Well, I'm infinitely indebted for the pipe, which I will inaugurate this evening, if I can get any smokable tobacco, and we will think over Johnny. You know, we shall pass through part of Switzerland and Germany on the way home, so you might get him something there—a pipe or a drinking-mug.'

' Dick shall get him a mug, and I will get him a pipe,' said Nora ; ' and you and I will get something for Dick, Mr. Cunningham.'

' We will.'

That evening, at the *table d'hôte*, Dick got into conversation with a German officer who was on his travels, and spoke English, somewhat bookish in form and odd in construction and pronunciation, but fairly fluent and intelligible, and they seemed to take to one another, and compared notes on attack formations and company columns, using the matches and toothpicks and square lumps of sugar to make diagrams after dinner with great enthusiasm. When they ordered a second bottle of Vino Rosso Commune, and lit cigars, Cunningham said to Nora :

' He seems to be fairly well occupied and amused. What do you say to coming to the post, and perhaps getting him a little present of some sort on the way back ? It is a splendid evening.'

And he waited for her reply in tremu-

lous anxiety, though outwardly cool enough.
She did not look at him, but said :

'Very well : I'll tell him we are going to
the post.'

Dick nodded on the receipt of the information, and went on about the distance of
the Reserves from the Supports in extended
order, and the files of direction. Nora
went to put on her hat and gloves, and
Cunningham went down to the entrance-hall
and waited.

After what seemed an interminable time
—about six minutes in reality, for Nora
was always deliberate, especially about really
important things, such as hats—she came
slowly downstairs, buttoning gloves, and
they went out and walked up the Merceria
and the angular alleys leading to that in-
geniously-concealed and dingy resort called
the post-office, where gondolas with water
postmen were waiting for parcels in the
black sucking water of a narrow canal.
This time there really were some letters.

'You put them in your pocket,' said

Nora, 'and we can read them when we get home in the light.'

'Very good. They will keep a little longer now, I dare say. Now come and take a look at Venice by night. Where would you like to go, just for a few minutes?'

'Oh, you know best. I'll go where you like. But we won't be long?'

'No.'

And they went on the Rialto, and looked up and down the canal, into the sparkling darkness of Venice. It was a dark night with bright stars, and the dim palaces could just be distinguished from the sky; while lights shone, yellow and irregular, in different directions, some steady as stars on the land, some moving like fire-flies on the water.

'Have you ever seen a night like this before?' said Cunningham.

'No, never.'

'Different from the Piazza, with the crowd and the cafés, isn't it? This is silent, ancient, ghostly Venice, now the busy and noisy people are all gone pleasuring, and there is peace and solitude. The air is full of memories of a great city and time and people, with statesmen, heroes, merchants, Moors, Jews, and noble ladies— all gone with the greatness of Venice— gone where Babylon and Troy town are, to an eternal home in man's memory.'

Nora said nothing. They were standing at one side of the bridge, and occasionally they heard the patter of some woman's wooden heels behind them, or the tramp of a soldier or two, but very few passengers went by at this time.

Cunningham looked at her. The place was poorly lit, but there was just light enough on the part of the Rialto where they stood to see one another. Then he said :

'Well, it's your turn to talk now. What are you thinking ?'

'I am thinking of several things. Do you remember you said this afternoon that

I had a natural appreciation of beautiful things, of places and pictures, and so on, and that I could easily learn things if I took the trouble ?'

' Yes, I said that.'

' And did you mean it ?'

' I meant everything I said to you this afternoon ; and I mean it still.'

Nora looked at him with a little smile, and replied :

' Then I wish you would teach me some things. There will be plenty of opportunity when we are back in England, and I shall want an occupation ; but I should like it to be holidays till we go back.'

' I will do anything in the world you like, possible or otherwise. But there is one thing you have taught me, even in this delightful holiday,' he continued (his heart thumping, ' fit to shake the Rialto down,' he thought to himself), ' which I don't think I shall forget.'

' Oh, what's that, then ?'

' Can't you imagine ?'

' No.'

And she shook her head, with a grave face and a malicious smile in her eyes.

' Come nearer, and I'll tell you.' She came nearer by about a hand's breadth. He took her hand again, and gently drew her nearer still and looked in her face. ' Don't you really know ?'

' No.'

And she smiled still more, as she shook her head with decision, but made no resistance at all when he put his disengaged arm round her ; indeed, she rather facilitated that movement by an apparently involuntary approach to him. And so they stood in the starlight, on the ancient bridge which leads to Fairyland.

And then he kissed her, and she shut her eyes and kissed him back.

' I don't think I need tell you what it is,' said he.

' And you have taught me something, too. I wonder if it's the same, at all ?'

' So do I.   Will you tell me ?'

'I don't think it had better be told. We'll each keep it a secret. Kiss me again, Mr. Cunningham.'

And Mr. Cunningham did.

'Now let's be getting home. There's somebody coming.'

'Very well. Take a look once more at the scene from the Rialto, and let us never forget it. But you needn't call me Mr. Cunningham, Nora dear. It is not necessary to be so respectful.'

'I didn't mean to be respectful, but I didn't know your other name.'

'Well, they christened me Andrew once, in the good old Kirk of Scotland. But it's a beastly name, I'll allow.'

'I shall call you chummy, I think—the way the soldiers do. There was Sergeant Dwyer, a friend of Dick's, and they used to pass a pipe one to another, and say, " Have a shaugh of mine, chummy !"'

'All right.' Then, as they came again into the swarming chattering crowd near the Piazza, Cunningham further said : ' What shall we say to Dick ?'

' Oh, nothing.   Let's see how long he'll be finding out.'

And they went into the hotel, and found that Dick had only just parted from the German officer, and was standing about waiting for them.

' Come along,' said Cunningham, ' to the Quadri.   I'm going to treat you children to-night.   We'll take a little walk about the Piazza first, and when we are tired of that we'll go upstairs and sample the Quadri's products.'

' I'm with you there.   That's a very clever fellow, and a fine soldier, that chap I've been talking to.   This is his card.'

And Cunningham read :

' KRÜGER,
Premier Lieutenant des 2ten. Schlesischen Infanterie—Reg. No. 84.

' I hope we haven't kept you waiting,' he said.

' Indeed no ! Have you got any letters?'

' Yes. They're in my pocket. We'll read them at our leisure. Come along.'

And they wandered out again. When they had perambulated the Piazza sufficiently, and laughed at Dick's attempts to blandish the eternal flower-women, they ascended to the first-floor of the Café Quadri, and took a light supper, with some extra-recommended Chianti, and discoursed merrily on their experiences of Continental travelling, and Dick, lifting his glass, said :

' And here's to the man that made the tour, and took the trouble, and worked the route, and took care of the baggage and commissariat, and had all the work that we might have all the fun, and we're having it. Here's to yourself, chummy !' and he drank.

Nora, looking across the table at Cunningham with malice aforethought, said, ' Here's to yourself, chummy !' and sipped some wine.

Dick looked at her, and then at him, and then grinned, but made no observation. What he thought was :

'There, I suppose they're after finding out what I've known these three weeks. More power !'

Then Cunningham said :

'You can't possibly have derived more joy from this wander of ours than I have, and I have to thank you for suggesting it.'

'Pass, grand rounds, and God save you kindly,' replied Dick. 'Now let's have a look at the letters.'

CHAPTER XXVI.

THERE were three letters from Redcliff and one from London. Of these, one was for Nora, and the other three for Cunningham. The one from London had been originally directed to him at the Rectory, Redcliff, and forwarded from there. This he recognised to be in Mrs. Denison's somewhat feeble handwriting (which was between that of a milliner and a young lady at a finishing school), and impatiently put it into his pocket to be read in private. The other two he saw to be from his uncle, Mr. Gilchrist, and from Johnny Smalley, respectively. He slit the envelopes of these open with a table-knife, and put them down and waited while Nora read hers aloud. It was from Jane, and ran as follows :

' " Dearest Nora, and Dear People generally,—Words fail to picture my relief on
hearing you were still to be found somewhere. I've been wishing you were here
ever since you left. It must be so jolly—I
mean, it must be a source of wild and
glamorous delight—to go about in a gondola
with Mr. Cunningham to quarrel with and
Dick to row you. Does he dress like a
gondolier ? I'm trying to get on with a
novel I'm writing, but I've hardly got the
spirit, everything is so at sixes and sevens,
especially sevens, and people are so aggra-
vating. My unhappy family is getting
almost more than I can manage. I do wish
you were all back here, and I had someone
with any sense to help me. I used to
think Johnny had some sense, but he's lost
it, and does nothing but hang after that
horrid woman." '

(' Now we are approaching the point,' said
Cunningham.)

' " She's just like the adventuresses in

the books, only they are generally a good
deal nicer ; and she drinks raw brandy after
dinner, and smells of tobacco.   Fräulein
says that's a French custom, and no harm
thought in it, though ' coot peer voss petter.'
And Johnny's always giving her expensive
presents.   She came across Fräulein and
me in the road the other day, and went
on as if I was a child with dolls.   Beast !
I told mamma, and she told me to never
mind, and not be silly, and attend to my
lessons.   Mamma can't understand that
anybody she and poor papa had accepted
could be viewed as anything but angels
by anybody else, and if you try and
make her see a thing she doesn't want to
see, she assumes a martyred expression, and
has to go and lie down.   Then I talked to
Johnny, and he was rather short-tempered.
I suppose he feels he is making a fool of
himself, and can't help it, and doesn't like
to be reminded of it.   He told me to mind
my own business.   He is like the old man

who, 'when they said he was wrong, merely
said "Bong!"' because he had no better
answer to make. I like Fräulein now I am
more grown up much better. She is a good
old sort, though she can't see a joke, and
she and Florrie are the only real allies I
have in 'this here most fatal go.' I wish
you were all here, for except the above,
who are not much use, I've no one to talk
to hardly, except people who look on
Mr. Scheiner as next door but one to a
cherubim, and her a sort of angel in the
latest fashion. Hélène's being rather silly
over him. I think he is making fun of her
sometimes, but she never sees it. She lurks
about in the garden and in muddy roads
just to meet him by accident, and Johnny
generally goes off to spend the afternoon
at the Riviera with that hateful woman,
and all the servants and the poor people,
and so on, talk about it. Oh dear, Nora,
I don't know what's going to become of us!
I should like to just run away to London
and live on my pen, and have Fräulein and

Florrie to keep house with me. I am afraid mamma rather likes them. You see, they flatter her and have a lot of money, and she won't listen to 'a child like me' when all the people here just worship the man.

'"I go and talk with old Barton—up the hill, you know; fell over the quarry. He is very shaky, and looks much older now, and his voice is higher and crackier; but he sticks to his rum, says he will never die ashore, and has the lowest possible opinion of Scheiner, which he expresses in emblematical talk. I suppose I ought not to go and gossip with a person like him, but his sympathy is refreshing, and he is old and lonely, and I'm beginning to feel old and lonely, too. My people are all taken up with these beastly foreigners, and Lilian's just the same as usual, putting everybody right and no use to anybody. Do come back soon.

'"Your affectionate cousin,

'"JANE.

' " P.S.—I nearly forgot.   Mr. Scheiner had a long talk in the library this morning with Johnny about investments.   I put Florrie on to listen at the door, and it seems he wants him to sell out something and put it into this Casino they're all cracked about, where he would get higher interest.   J. said he would think it over.   But that woman will make him do it, and I'm afraid there's something up.   I haven't read Gaboriau for nothing.   If she told Johnny to get all his teeth drawn and give them to Mr. Scheiner, he would do it.   I talked to old Barton this afternoon—of course I ought not, I know that—and he said I ought to have someone to help me, and that it was a man's job, and advised me to go and have a talk with ' Passon Gilchrist ' about it.   Then he said : 'And don't ye go frettin', my pretty.   We'm bound to get this yer putt right, if Hi 'as to go and cut that ' (emblematical talk) ' Partygee's liver out.'   I went to see Mr. Gilchrist, and he went to see old Barton, and then he told me he hardly knew what to advise, but would write to Mr. Cunningham. In the meantime, that man is to sing at an entertainment Mr. Disney is getting up for the New Church Completion Fund to-night, and we're all going in our best clothes. Excuse all this long and muddled letter, but I must tell somebody, and I hope you'll all come back soon. I expect Dick to bring me something very nice.

' " Yours,
' " JANE." '

'This is a queer start,' said Dick.

'Very,' replied Cunningham. 'But let me see if my uncle throws any further light on it, and then we'll consider the matter in a council of war.'

And he read Mr. Gilchrist's letter aloud, while the music played a cheerful polka in the Piazza outside, and the voices and footsteps made a murmuring accompaniment in the joyous Venetian night :

' " My dear Andrew,

' " I envy you your Southern tour, especially in such weather as we are now experiencing in these unfortunate isles. I should much like to see the land of Virgil and Dante, the blue skies, the olives and vines, and, perhaps, also Soracte glittering in the snow.

' " But I am afraid it is my duty to speak of more modern and less elevating matters. My attention has been directed—firstly, by little Miss Jane Smalley, who called on me in a state of excitement and distress for advice; secondly, by that singular old recluse who lives on Romer Down ; and finally, and that briefly, by the inevitable echoes of parish gossip which reach even me—to the doings of Mr. Leopold Scheiner and his wife, especially with reference to the Smalleys.

' " It seems that since the sudden and lamentable calling away of Mr. Smalley, the influence and intimacy of those foreigners has grown very much in that family, and it

is doubtful if that influence is for good.
Jane Smalley's pure instincts and childish
inexperience have combined to produce in
her a vague element of suspicion and alarm,
founded, I take it, more on personal dislike
than anything else, which it would scarcely
do to accept seriously as evidence. But the
old man who gives the name of Barton, who
has grown very infirm since his accident,
hinted to me of matters within his knowledge which, if other than the wanderings
of an enfeebled mind, place another and
most surprising aspect on things, as well as
leading me to fear that these persons are
not likely to do poor young Smalley—who
now has a large property at his disposal,
mind you—and his family any good. I am
an old man, and not conversant with the
world, or with the law, and the means of
making proper inquiries, and I should much
like to consult you, who are in possession of
those faculties I have mentioned, and might
be able to set your fingers at once on the
right course to be adopted, and perhaps

prevent some great wrong being done. The whole matter has surprised and upset me a great deal." '

(' Dear old man !' said Nora.)

' " I forward a letter from London, as it may perhaps be of importance, and remain,

' " Your affectionate old uncle,

' " JAMES GILCHRIST." '

' There'll be another surprise for him one of these days,' observed Dick, ' I was just after thinking.'

' And that ?' said Cunningham.

' Well, supposing, for instance, his affectionate nephew were to present him with a Papist niece-in-law ?   I only said supposing.'

' What's that you're saying ?' said Nora with attempted defiance and a fine scarlet colour.

Dick chuckled, and replied :

' Oh, nothing.   Only Dick Scanlan's not quite such a fool as he is taken for, me lady. What do you say, Cunningham ?'

' True bill.'

Dick held out his strong hand across the table to Cunningham, and said :

' God bless you, chummy, and make both your years long and your lives happy ! Now let's get back to business.'

' This last letter,' said Cunningham, ' appears to be from the representative of the defendants.

' " DEAR OLD FRAUD,

' " I like the way you are spending the Michaelmas term. Find Ethics grow luxuriantly on the banks of the Grand Canal ? Getting a trifle Home-Ruly in general tone, and punctuated with shamrocks, aren't they ? I imagine Italy would be the right place to be in with the right people. I should like to converse with you quietly over tobacco on these and many matters. No one here to talk to with any mind or sense. Even Jane, who used to have more sense than the rest of my family put together, is turning narrow-minded and *bornée*, and moons about in a lonesome way with that addle-brained conglomerate of separable and irregular verbs she calls Frowlein. Perhaps she misses a military man with a Dublin brogue. Otherwise, I don't know what's the matter. I'm doing pretty well on the whole. It's a fiendish bore, being looked on as a head of a family and owner of property. People have become so deadly respectful all of a sudden, and they will call, and I have to call back, in the waggonette with Mrs. Podsnap. When I want refuge from the hopeless *banalité* and general mudsomeness of Redcliff, I sometimes seek it in the company of Kitty Scheiner, who, you will remember, is a wonderfully clever as well as an attractive person, though, I fancy, snorted at by some of the unco' guid here because alien or Catholic, or well dressed, or some other rot of the usual Redcliff type. However, I don't pay the smallest attention to anybody's gossip or prejudice, as you can imagine. Only too thankful to find a rational person to talk to. He's a thundering good sort, too, though ape-like at times. Greet dear old Dick and Nora for me. Greet Syncritus, and all the other Johnnies. And accept my best curse.

   ' " Thine, weary and dubious, and cumbered with much business,

                ' " JOHN SMALLEY." '

' Poor Johnny !' said Nora.

' There are rather too many French words in that letter,' said Cunningham. ' Now then, my friends. Let us consider this matter. Let us light fresh Virginias, Dick, and fill the glasses. Nora, while we are trying to make these fireworks kindle, you might give us your opinion.'

' I think Jane is right, and that Mrs. Scheiner is not a nice woman at all.'

' Question is, what's to be done ?' said Dick.

' Now, look here,' said Cunningham, ' just let us get this thing clear first of all. Does any one of us three believe in this Scheiner as an honest man (which is what he pretends

to be), and as disinterested as — say, as
Johnny himself?'

'Well, I know nothing against him,' said
Dick candidly, 'and he's always been pleasant
to us.   Still, it looks a little bad when your
uncle thinks it worth while to write about it,
and it's against a man when Jane doesn't
like him.'

'I never liked the woman,' said Nora,
'and I don't trust the man.   I'll tell you
something, Dick, you don't know.   At that
ball, when poor Mr. Smalley died, this Mr.
Scheiner wanted me to let him have a lot of
money—we spoke of a thousand pounds—as a
subscription for the cause of Irredentism,
and I was such a fool then that I would
have asked you for the money, and most
likely you would have given me a cheque
without asking a question, only my chummy
here interfered, and prevented it.   I lost
my temper at the time, and made a holy
show of myself; but I was glad afterwards
you didn't let me do it,' she said, turning
to Cunningham, 'and I know he got

some money from that boy, little Satterthwaite.'

'*She* worked that youth, I think,' said
Cunningham. 'He tried Nora with the ingenious pretext that William O'Mara was
working this Irredenta bosh with him. I
said that most likely William O'Mara was
doing nothing of the kind; but if he were, it
was no reason for subscribing, and I offered
to ascertain.'

'Well I never !' said Dick ; 'and why
wouldn't you tell me this, Nora ?'

'Oh, I was ashamed of the whole thing,
and, after all, nothing was done.'

'Scheiner knew jolly well why too,' said
Cunningham, 'and, if you can judge by expression, has entered my name in a book,
with a large black mark to it.'

'But what's he wanting with all this
money ?' said Dick ; 'he's rich enough.'

'How do you know ?' said Cunningham.
'What does anybody know about him be-
yond the fact that he lives in good style ?
How do you know he is rich at all ? Or

that his name isn't Moses? I tell you all Redcliff, except Mr. Satterthwaite, who is a man of business and rigid principles, took him entirely on trust.'

' Well, now, you're the learned man and the counsellor,' said Dick, ' you just reel out the case to us according to your understanding of it, and we'll listen, and give you our opinion, and then we'll decide what to do.'

' Yes, you tell us what you really think,' said Nora.

' Exactly. First take the facts. This man comes to Redcliff, and gives himself out as a wealthy and luxurious person, and spends, perhaps, from four to five hundred pounds in living at a hotel, entertaining, and making himself popular. Although a clever fellow, he lets himself be rushed for subscriptions right and left, and, generally speaking, could not be more obviously bidding for popularity if he were a candidate for Parliament. He proceeds to become most intimate, or to try to be, with the people who he gathers are the best off, in point of property or money. He carefully advertises his connection with this Irredentist bosh, which he is far too sharp to care a twopenny curse about in reality, but knows will go down as interesting romance with most of the people there, who, of course, know nothing whatever about it, and may safely be told the first nonsense which comes into his head.'

'Don't be nasty now!' from Nora.

'Next, he is seen in the early morning giving money, silver too, to an obscure old vagabond who happens to have turned up in the neighbourhood. If it were benevolence, it was too large a sum to give at a time and place at which no one was likely to see it done. He was more in the habit of advertising his benevolence than doing it in the dark.'

'Who saw that?' asked Dick.

'My uncle, the Rector. Yes, I think we're getting on. If it wasn't benevolence, what was it? I say, as the only conclusion common-sense and knowledge of the world leaves open, Blackmail. He is afraid of this old loafer. Next, this old man falls down a deep quarry and swears someone pushed him over. By a lucky chance he is not killed. You know all about that. Then he got poor Mr. Smalley, who, with all respect, was not a clever man, to involve himself in some investment juggle, by which Mr. Smalley wins some fifty pounds. Sprat, I take it, to catch a herring, if not cod or whale. Then a woman turns up from nowhere. He says she is his wife. Heaven knows who she is in reality. She speaks French very well, I know, better than he does, and they were both talking it to one another at that ball, in rather a disputatious manner, and using what I can only describe as " language," such as should not occur between ladies and gentlemen in any country. She does not, in a general way, behave at all like a modest, well-conducted married woman, though the Redcliffites, in blind faith in money and " side," put it all down to " foreign " eccentricity, as if ladies

and decent women in all countries would not
be distinguished from the other thing.'

'I think you're right about her,' said
Nora.

'What business has this woman to per-
petually entertain poor Johnny, who is ten
years younger than she in age, and twenty
in experience, by herself, at the Riviera?
What would be thought of it if she were a
poor woman, with beauty, and not foreign?
Then this man, ladies and gentlemen of the
jury, is always apparently on the make or
look-out for money. The Casino Company
and the Cretan Loan are only Irredentism
on a larger scale, the fable narrated with the
name changed. Do you know, Nora, why
you never heard any more about that
subscription?'

'No, I do not.'

'I'll tell you. I met the Scheiner man
one day, casually, on the esplanade, after
I'd been bathing, and I told him I hoped he
would allow me to make a small contribution
to the sacred cause as soon as I had received

a reply to my letter to my friend William
O'Mara on the subject.   It was only a try
on, because I don't know that statesman to
speak to, and had not written to him at all,
but it worked beautifully.   Did you ever see
a cobra draw back its head and flatten out
its cheeks to strike ?   Well, he looked like
that.   Then he thanked me politely.   He's
got plenty of presence of mind, that party,
and he is getting quite fond of me, I think.'

'It's all beginning to look like Queer
Street,' said Dick ;   'but about Johnny ?'

'Well, Johnny's got a lot of property.
Woman to act as decoy—old story.   She
might even ruin his life for ever, which
would be worse than losing the money.
Besides, there are those girls and his mother
to be thought of.   Do you follow me ?'

'I do,' said Dick ;   'but there's no actual
crime against the man, as far as I can see.'

'Quite so.   There is only presumption,
and the facts, as we know them, don't carry
us beyond presumption.   But I propose,
now things are getting so unexpectedly

critical for that infatuated Johnny, to find out a lot more facts. I am afraid it is my duty to start off for England as soon as possible, though I know it is rather hard to leave you now we are all so jolly comfortable.'

'Leave us ! Don't you think we're coming, too ?' said Nora.

' 'Are you ?'

'We are not going to leave you to have all the trouble by yourself, chummy,' she replied, 'you may be quite sure of that—don't you think so, Dick ?'

'Faith I do ! We'll back him up. And we'll bucket out Scheiner with the bay'net and the butt, before he gets hold of Johnny's property.'

'It is well. Then, if we are going, and want to do it with some regard to comfort, as well as to speed, the sooner we do it the better. I don't apprehend that a crisis will come in the course of the next two or three days. I suppose they will try and work Johnny up to the Casino rot ; but they will

require time for that, and even if he con-
sented to sell some of his property, that
couldn't be done like selling a pound of tea.
Still, there's nothing like being on the safe
side.   Wherefore I ask, can you be ready
to go to-morrow ?'

'Oh yes,' said Nora.   'I will not be long
packing.'

'I'm always ready for any time the
route's given me,' said Dick.

'You are.   Then we will go to Milan
to-morrow, sleep there, and take the train
in the morning *viâ* Chiasso and the St.
Gothard tunnel.   That will get us to Basel
in the evening, so you will see a fair glimpse
of Switzerland—mind, it will be much colder
on the other side of the St. Gothard tunnel
—then from Basel we can get through
France to Calais, so you'll have the advantage of passing through a couple of new
countries.   We will go as quickly, however,
as we can, consistently with tolerable comfort.
Then, when we get to Redcliff, we'll hear
what Jane has to say, and what my uncle

has to say, and I might perhaps then find it well to do a private remonstrance with Johnny. If that has no result, I must have searching inquiries made about the gentleman and the lady.'

' Supposing we don't find anything about them ?' said Dick.

' Then we can't help it. We shall have done our best, and that at some personal sacrifice, and things must take their course. But I have a pretty strong impression that we shall find something against them. I thought the man was a sharper from the first, though of course I had no evidence, and when his charming wife came, that opinion was strengthened. It's a great nuisance, though, to have our tour cut short in this way, because Johnny will be such a fool.'

' Perhaps we'd better go home now and go to bed,' suggested Dick. And the suggestion was adopted.

When Cunningham was alone in his own room, he read the other letter, Mrs. Deni-

son's.   It consisted mostly of regrets for his
absence, allusions to her loneliness, and semi-
interrogative suggestions about ' some girl,'
whose society she assumed Cunningham to be
enjoying.   It had no particular point, or
intention of any intelligible kind, but expressed the strong affection of a weak mind,
and as such was pathetic.   Cunningham
himself, in the fever and dazzle of his
triumph with Nora, was nearly blind to this
other poor soul's attachment to him, which
he had neither suspected nor invited ; but
even he read somewhat between these lines
—lines of veiled suffering and love, though
in penny novelette style, and shaky in the
spelling—and he was sorry.

But one sentence caught his attention for
other reasons.   It was this :

' . . . It happened last Wednesday I
met my long-lost husband face to face in a
hansom.   I mean he was in a hansom, with
a bag on the top, and I was walking in the
Strand, just for something to do, and he
came round the corner of Wellington Street.

I suppose he was coming from Waterloo Station. I didn't quite know him at first ; but there was a block in the traffic, and he had to stop a long time, and I had a good look at him. I took jolly good care he didn't see me. He looks a little older, and has his hair a little touched with gray now, and he is better dressed. I expect he's got in some soft place again, and is going to marry some other poor fool of a girl. . . .'

' That photo ; Waterloo ; Wednesday,' mused Cunningham. ' I must see that photo again. I must find out if Scheiner went to town last Wednesday. It's a shot. It's not wholly a shot, either. I always thought his face reminded me of something. And so to bed.'

CHAPTER XXVII.

At Redcliff the English climate was displaying its striking powers of variation, more particularly an ingenious alternation of frost and thaw combined with snow and rain, which made the country ankle-deep in slush one day, and one immense slide the next. The frost was rarely hard or persistent enough for skating, but quite sufficient to make the horses fall down, and to burst the pipes, while the mild intervening weather lasted just long enough to relax human tonicities and adapt constitutions for the reception of colds, neuralgia, bronchitis, and rheumatism, when the inevitable ' change ' came. The one thing constant among these variants was the sea-fog, and day and night were saddened by the hootings of distant steamers, and the weird banshee-like performance of the siren at the lighthouse.

The Redcliff Casino and Winter-garden Company had been established for some time. President, the Earl of Croagh-patrick; Vice-Presidents, the Marquis di Bórso-vuoto, Sir Atkinson Gooch, D.L., J.P., etc., Reginald Paynter, Esq., J.P., the Worshipful the Mayor, J.P., and the rest of them. Johnny Smalley held a few shares, but had not yet made up his mind to qualify himself as a vice-president by increasing his holding to the required amount. There were plenty of shareholders at present, many of them naturally persons dwelling in the neighbourhood, tradesmen and others who hoped to profit in various ways by the new undertaking, especially those connected with the art of building and letting houses.

The piece of ground for the establish-ment had been selected, and marked out with neat little red flags on white sticks. It was a good-sized oblong *terrain*, on Romer Down, commanding a magnificent view both of the sea, the bay, and the Cove of Roylieu on the further side, and swept by healthy, bracing breezes in summer, while in winter the glass winter-garden, with its groves of palms and aloes on the south side of the establishment, would completely shelter the occupant, and at the same time permit him to enjoy the view. This plot of ground contained within its limits the *taudis* occupied by Mr. Isaac Barton, who scoffed openly at the whole thing, and swore (literally) that, old as he was, he would live to see the last of it.

The secretary of this projected Stately Pleasure Dome was Leopold Henry Scheiner, Esq., and the vice-presidents had had up to the present but one serious task, that of voting their own salaries, and that of 'our most able and indefatigable secretary, whose tireless exertions leave no stone unturned which may render our edifice more solid, no path untrodden which may lead us, and with us civilization, into higher realms and vaster successes,' to use the picturesque language of the noble president.

Johnny had been induced with some difficulty to postpone becoming a vice-president and investing in the scheme on a scale so large as to involve realizing some of the property at Portsmouth in order to find the money, for not only was he very much under the influence of the Scheiners —that is to say, of Mrs. Scheiner—but also pressed by his own family to ' take the matter up,' and ' go into it more seriously,' to ' really pay more attention to business matters,' and so on, and this and that, different little persuasive pin-pricks and gentle goadings. It is, however, extremely likely that the above promptings on the part of his family were as instrumental as anything might be in preventing him from taking the decisive step. When a young man of a certain temperament is contem-plating a project, he is hardly human if

he does not regard that project with less
enthusiasm after his mother and sisters
have urged its merits on him. Mrs. and
the Misses Smalley's reasons for support-
ing the scheme were these : first, that they
believed (without the smallest knowledge
of the subject, or any evidence whatever)
that the results would be fabulously profitable, and that Scheiner was a very rich
and successful financial genius, because he
said so ; second, because the Gooches and
an earl were ' in it.'

There were, however, in Redcliff three
old men who had in their different ways
strongly warned Johnny against the scheme,
and though not wholly free from the pre-
judices of Rehoboam on the subject of
counsellors, he could not but be impressed
to some degree, and when Cunningham returned, Johnny was hardly surprised to find
his old friend on the same side as the three
old men of Redcliff who refused to make
obeisance to the golden image which Scheiner
had set up. And these were : Mr. Gilchrist,

the Rector ; old Mr. Satterthwaite, the man
of business, politician and Puritan; and Isaac
of the Isle of Wight, sometime mariner, and
fabricator of strange tales. Each of these,
in his different style and language, strongly
warned Johnny to leave it alone, and all
stated that they had good reasons for what
they said, as would probably appear as time
went on without their active interference.
Cunningham suggested to Johnny simply
to wait until a few inquiries had been made,
to which Johnny agreed, and then Cunningham went straight to call on Mr. Satterthwaite, with whom he had a prolonged
interview, resulting in his departure to
London.

In the meantime, let us give our attention for awhile to what may be termed in
legal language the ' other side.' The ' other
side ' may be taken as embodied in the
three persons in the private parlour apper-
taining to the Scheiner suite of apartments
at the Riviera Hotel. They no longer took
an interest in the French windows opening

on to the balcony facing the sea.   On the
contrary, those windows were carefully
shuttered and the curtains drawn, while
the tiled hearth blazed with a good coal fire
supplemented by logs of split-up wreckage.
Close to the fire sat Scheiner, leaning
forward with his elbows on his knees, looking like a chilly and rather sullen monkey.
In the armchair on the opposite side sat
Kitty, in a gorgeous winter tea-gown of
shot heliotrope velvet, trimmed with brown
fur, embroidering an ' L ' on a crimson silk
pocket - handkerchief with skilful little
fingers.   Up and down the room, smoking
cigarettes, stopping occasionally to make
his remarks more emphatic, sipping occasionally at a little glass of brandy which
stood, with other little glasses, grouped
round a little decanter on a little table
before the fire, marched the Earl of
Croaghpatrick, with a local newspaper in
his hand.

'Look at this, Leo.   I told you when
the first par. came out that there was some-

body behind it, and you had better ascertain who. What did you do ? Nothing.'

'I tell you it's as simple as A B C. It's just *chantage*. The paper wants to be squared, that's all.'

'I say it is not simple at all. Your idea of accounting for things is to adopt the first commonplace that comes into your head, avoid taking any trouble, and then assume everything is all right because you have said it is.'

'What's the trouble ?' asked Kitty.

'Why,' began Leo, 'it's simply this—I'll put the thing for you in a nutshell : There is a paper—a weekly paper—here ; I hadn't heard of it, and didn't know what its political views were——'

'Just what you ought to have found out,' interjected the Earl of Croaghpatrick with grim calmness.

'But last week it had this in it : " The Proposed Redcliff Casino.—We should like to know the state of the accounts, and what proportion the capital expended bears to the

actual progress of this scheme, which we
have always conscientiously opposed as at
least a foolish extravagance, and at worst a
means of moral and political corruption, re-
producing all the worst features of the
Primrose League." Well, it seems to be a
Radical paper. Then the last number has
this : " The Casino Scandal. — From the
silence with which our last remarks on this
extremely objectionable project have been
received, we are led to fear that there is
something worse to be revealed than the
making of profits out of human frivolity and
vice by some of our prominent fellow-towns-
men and residents who ought to know
better, and have higher views of their
duties as citizens, gentlemen, and Christians,
and to remember that in these days of
democracy the people no longer have their
voices stifled, or are to be intimidated by
rank and wealth from enforcing, sternly if
necessary, the principles of their own manly,
simple, and yet vigorous morality." '

' So the British Democracy is manly,

simple, and vigorously moral,' observed the
Earl. ' It's nice to know that. Go on, Leo.'

' " It is much to be apprehended that
some of our aristocratic neighbours above
alluded to have fallen into the pit which
they digged for others, and have been led
by the greed of gain to become the ignorant
victims and tools of a gang of booby-catchers
far sharper than themselves, who have used
the various means of seduction to which
human frailty is susceptible for their own
private ends. We say no more at present,
but we are fully conscious of our responsi-
bilities as an organ of enlightened public
opinion." That is all.'

' Jolly, isn't it, Kitty ? Leo and I are a
" gang of booby-catchers," and I suppose
you are politely alluded to as one of the
" means of seduction to which human frailty
is susceptible." Moreover, you may be
perfectly certain that that paper has been
sent with the par. underlined to all our
venerable band of vice-presidents, who will
be pleased.'

' It's perfectly horrid !' said Kitty.
' What are we to do ?'

' What we ought to do, and what the goodly fellowship of boobies will want, is to bring an action for libel, and that is not a course I can safely accept or plausibly repudiate. It is becoming evident that things must soon come to a crisis. Either we must have a lot more capital to replace what has been expended on—well, on expenses, or we must disappear, shoot the moon, do a guy, as the picturesque slang of the period puts it.'

' But, my dear Crow,' exclaimed Scheiner, jumping up and spreading out and opening and shutting his hands, ' what have we to be ashamed of ? We have been perfectly straight and open about the thing—selected the site, paid the quarterly dividend, and everything ! Let's bring the libel action, and the paper will be glad to buy us off.'

' What's the good of talking that rubbish to me ? You know that I've used a good deal of the money, you've spent a good deal more on yourself—you're an awfully expensive animal to keep, Leo—and the dividends and salaries to directors, and blackmail to financial journalists, have come out of capital.'

' Where should they come from ?'

' *Sanctissima simplicitas !* Where indeed ? But you can't very well present accounts to a court of justice, or a receiver in bankruptcy either, in which the bulk of the expenditure would appear in the form of champagne, flowers for the buttonhole, new suits of clothes, shirts, and pairs of yellow boots for Leopold Henry Scheiner, Esq. My dear fellow, try and realize that it means Holloway !'

' Kitty's had the money !' exclaimed Leo angrily.

' Now, don't be a hound, Leo,' replied Crow, calmly expelling smoke from his nostrils. ' The " woman whom Thou gavest me " apology is about the dirtiest on record. You spent the money mostly on yourself— you always do when you have got any—and you have run up no end of bills, I don't doubt; and I don't blame you, for I do the same. But don't go and pretend you don't. And please realize that you have to share trouble and risk as well as pleasure and profit in this here most fatal go.

' It seems to me, Crow, you are taking a great deal too much of the bossing of this show on your shoulders. Look here, who invented the whole thing ? who suggested it ? who got up the meetings, and got you into a soft thing, and a thing that will be a great big honest Boom, with Knighthoods and Garters and all sorts of things in it ? And just because a miserable little paper, instigated by some envious reptile who hasn't got a contract or something, throws a mud-pellet at us, you want to back down and run away, and talk as if we were em- barked in a criminal plot ! Why, I love this Casino ! I mean it to go ! I want to make this horrible, tepid, paltry little Eng- lish provincial museum of antiquities and commonplaces into a bright place of pleasure, with music, and fashion, and dresses, and *tintamarre*, and beauty, and youth——'

'—— And Conversation Kenge, latter part (by request) by L. Scheiner, Esq. At the same time, I repeat that we are within measurable distance of Holloway, unless we can get a largish contribution on the quiet from somebody. All that enthusiasm of yours is quite right in its proper place, Leo, and it may take *you* in, but it doesn't me. And I tell you so again, for the last time, and you know it's true. So look about you. Find out who's at the back of that paper, and what his reason is. Postpone the general meeting as long as possible. I must be off now and catch the up-express.'

' Where are you going ?'

' I'm going to the south of France for the good of my health, and to see if I can't pull off a good thing at a certain Casino where youth and beauty, and age and ugliness, and music and fashion and brightness, and all your bag of tricks, are already collected.'

'There comes into my mind a disagree-
able old saying about rats leaving a ship.'

'There comes into mine one about rogues
falling out. Ta - ta ! Good luck ! Wire
will fetch me from the Continental in about
thirty hours, I believe. Good-bye, Kitty.
Merry Christmas !'

And Crow got into his great fur over-
coat, and was subsequently taken to the
station in the hotel 'bus, with great rever-
ence and tender care. 'Jove !' he reflected,
' hope it won't be Black Maria, instead of
the Riviera 'bus, one of these days. That
Leo is making a deadly mess of a capital
thing, as usual. I wonder Kitty sticks to
him so well. Wonderful little woman !
Wonderful man, to have so many good ideas,
and be so incapable of carrying them out !
It'll end in Kitty keeping him—it's pretty
near it already, I suspect. Poor little
woman !' And he lit a cigarette, put his
feet on the hot-water tin, and proceeded to
read a sporting paper.

As soon as he was gone, Leo Scheiner said :

'Now I'm going to talk! Crow's a nuisance at times, but he's partly right, I'm afraid. Satterthwaite is at the back of that paper, as I know perfectly well. We have got to get money somehow. There is a row coming, if we are not careful, and Crow knows it, and has bolted. That's one thing. Then, I wonder what made those people return again so soon ? It looks odd, but I do not quite see what should bring them back.'

'What does it matter, any way ?'

'It matters a great deal to us. That man Cunningham is going smelling about, and interfering with everything. He will never be satisfied till he has done some mischief or other. He has a good deal of influence with that boy of yours, for example.'

'He will not do any harm there, I'm quite sure.'

'Yes, but your certainty is not to be depended on.   Half of it is simple vanity.'

'You are in a very unpleasant temper this afternoon, Leo.'

'That is very possible.   It seems to me that you do not realize that we are running a very serious risk in this affair.'

'Who invited you to undertake this affair ?   You did it entirely on your own responsibility, without telling me more than you could help, and you got me to join you because you thought you could not do without me.   Have I not backed you up and faithfully carried out your ideas ?   It is no pleasure to me.   I am pretty sick of making a fool of that boy, if it comes to that.   He is quite a nice boy, and I sometimes feel inclined to tell him he ought to be ashamed of himself for worshipping a wretched fraud of a woman nearly ten years older than himself.'

'Ah !   And why do you not tell him so ?'

'Because, Leo, I am carrying out the

orders of an ungrateful man called Scheiner, whom I am still fool enough to be fond of. I can't think of any better reason.'

' Well, well, be cheerful. Take a glass of brandy. We will best them all yet. Now listen, and I will put you *au courant* with the latest developments. Perhaps I was unreasonable to blame you for what is merely the fault of circumstances.'

' I imagine you were. Well ?'

' I was standing in the hall of the Club yesterday, making myself agreeable to the new doctor who has taken old Wheeler's practice. One should always be agreeable to doctors and priests and parsons of all kinds. Why ? Because they both spend their time circulating gossip among all the families in the place, especially the old women, and they are useful advertisers, because people believe what their clergy and their doctors say, and repeat it. This doctor is the originator of the Redcliff Spa, having been here on a previous occasion when old Wheeler went for a holiday, and dug up some drain, probably. He has had up till quite recently a practice in the middle of London in a rather poor neighbourhood, and has had enough of it, so when old Wheeler arranged to retire, Hanlon arranged to succeed him. Hanlon is the new man's name, a cheerful, talking, foolish, fat little Irishman. Thinks himself clever, and is simple. I very soon reckoned him up. Good. I say we were in the hall of the Club. That very useful man, Paynter, introduced us. Paynter is always in a state of alarm about the condition of his inside or something equally interesting, so of course he knows the doctor. As we are conversing, there comes in friend Cunningham with a brown leather bag. He has on a long ulster, and carries a rug and umbrella. He places the bag and rug in the charge of the porter, saying he will call for them later on, and is about to pass out again with the umbrella, when he sees Paynter and me, to whom he nods, and emits one of those murmuring alalisms which an Englishman uses when he thinks he is being polite. Paynter, seeing the man is in a hurry, detains him, out of pure stupidity, and asks him questions about his uncle's health. That is one of the reasons why I call Paynter a useful man. Here my friend Herr Doctor Hanlon recognises my friend, my dear friend Cunningham, and says: "Ah, how are you?" Cunningham looks a little surprised, but accepts the recognition, and replies that his health is reasonable, considering the climate. The doctor then adds: "And how is the little chap and his mamma?" pronouncing the word "mamma" in the way peculiar to Irish persons.'

'My! this begins to be quite interesting.'

'My friend Cunningham looks at him for a moment, and says: "Who do you mean?" Then he adds, "Oh yes, of course. I was thinking of something else. They are quite well, thank you."

'"I wasn't indiscreet now?" says the

doctor, with an arch grin, for which I wonder Cunningham didn't lay him out.

' " Not at all," says Cunningham, as cool as the thermometer, and then he nods and goes away. The useful man, Paynter, was listening with all his long ears, I need hardly say. I made the doctor tell us a little more, with the aid of some whisky and a cigar, Paynter staying, of course, for the pleasure of getting loaded up with fresh gossip. Paynter is now going round Redcliff like the man who rings a bell and shouts " God save the Queen ! Lost, a tin locket, in High Street." I learn that there is a lady in London and a little boy, that Mr. Cunningham is interested in them, and —that is really all ; but I am taking measures to ascertain all the facts. That bag and rug meant London. Leaving them at the Club means that he is going to visit the Scanlans first, and then take a later train.'

' He is engaged to the Scanlan woman.'

'So it is reported. So much the

better, for there will be all the bigger
row !'

' What's the good of all this ?'

' It will detach the Scanlans from Cunningham. They are naturally destitute of
brains. It is only he who keeps them in a
suspicious state, and tells them what they
ought to do, like a nurse taking care of a
pair of children. Let them only mistrust
and quarrel with him, and I will work them
like wax. Besides, it will amuse me to
puff a little dart with a little poisoned tip
into my friend Cunningham.'

' I will not have you making love to that
woman, Leo !' suddenly replied Kitty, with
a reflection of the fire in her brown eyes,
which young Satterthwaite had not un-
happily described as sherry-coloured.

' Ah !' said Leo through his nose and
between his teeth, ' what woman ?'

' That Scanlan woman, whom you went
to see when you had told me you were
going to the Club for the afternoon a day
or two ago.'

' Who told you that ?'

' No one ; but I know it.'

' Supposing it to be true, what of it ? It is absurd to make such scenes. You do not object to my making love to Hélène Smalley ; I do not object to your doing the same with Johnny, and with General Barker and Mr. Paynter, too, if you like !'

' Yes, provided they gave me bracelets and fans and things for you to pawn later on in London, you wouldn't mind my flirting with the devil and all his angels ! That's you, all the way !'

' Once for all, what is the use of talking like this ? You have a comfortable place to live in, good things to eat, wine to drink, beautiful, magnificent, expensive clothes to wear, seductive personal charms, no work to do, and several men to admire you. What in misery *do* you want ?'

' I want you not to make love to that woman. That is what you mean. That is what you really want to get Cunningham *brouillé* with them for. Hélène Smalley don't make any difference, because she is a harmless fool, but this other woman——'

' Well, what about this other woman ?'

' She may be a fool, too—probably is—but not harmless. I know t'other from which, mind you, Leo! I have not had all my experience for nothing, and I tell you that she is the only woman in this God-forsaken hole except me—the others are all sawdust dolls ; and you know that as well as I do !'

' I wish you could understand that my one motive and aim is to make money for you and me to spend, when we are far away from here, and can laugh at all these absurd quarrels, and enjoy ourselves really, somewhere where the narrow rules of chattering fools of a little tin-pot English provincial society do not prevail ; and in carrying out that motive I am giving no attention to anything else—certainly not to women, unless they happen to be instrumental !'

' That's all very fine, but you take care not to make that particular woman too instrumental, or there'll be a row !'

Kitty was standing before him with her arms down at full length at her sides, but the fists turned upwards and outwards.

'I think you are forgetting yourself. When you have had rather too much brandy you get dreadfully irritable and talk nonsense. You revert to an inferior type, which is not attractive, and is unworthy of a woman of your attainments.'

In response to this moral lecture, Kitty, who had perhaps been taking rather too frequent *petits verres* in the course of this exciting conversation, broke into a long and rapid speech in which there was little perceptible of logic, but a fine display of temper. When she had finished, Scheiner said :

'Well, what is the use of all that? It makes no change in things, and it makes a painful exhibition of you. You had better go and lie down.'

She then proceeded to weep hysterically, and ask him to forgive her. He replied magnanimously :

'There is nothing to forgive. You are certainly not quite mistress of yourself, and had better go and lie down. I will call you in time for dinner, and you will then have forgotten all this.'

She went away silently, conquered for the time by the cold-blooded selfishness of her husband and by her own feelings. When she had gone, Leo ground his teeth and shook his fists at the door through which she had departed, and remarked :

'A little more of this, *mein süsses Herz*, and you will be requested to return to the streets and gutters from which you came, and find some other fool to feed you !'

Then he warmed himself, and went to the piano, and began to sing, ' Du bist wie eine Blume.'

If Leo Scheiner's thoughts had been acts just then, it is probable that several persons would have met with far from painless extinction. However, after soothing himself with the sweet melody of his own voice, and the contemplation in the glass of his

own face, which he proceeded to deck
with an almost conical, rather dandified
Astrakhan cap, he put on his goloshes, his
fur-lined coat, turned the collar up, and
went out. Snow had been falling all the
afternoon and was falling still, and there
was a thin, half-melted layer of it upon the
ground. A few dim, hurrying figures were
visible in the dismal flickering whiteness of
the High Street of Redcliff, but no doubt
the immense majority of the population
were in their houses taking tea in front
of fires. Leo Scheiner looked at the large
shop where stationery, photographs of the
locality, oxidized silver frames, brass ink-
stands, and wooden paper-knives stained by
the Redcliff mineral spring were sold, where
also a post-office and library were established, and through the windows, dim with
condensed moisture, perceived vague forms
engaged in turning over and over confused
heaps of Christmas cards in trays, and he
reflected upon the infinite dreariness of an
English Christmas, the foolish pictures and

stories in the illustrated 'numbers,' the family gatherings, the forced hilarity, the great gashed, gaping red joint of beef, the plum-pudding, the crackers with paper hats in them, the comic-paper-cum-servants'-hall witticisms about the mistletoe.

'Oh, it is an awful country to live in in winter!' he concluded as he walked on in the direction of The Oaks, where the Scanlans lived, and asked if they were at home.

Being answered in the affirmative, he took off his goloshes and handed his fur coat and cap to the servant (retired Sergeant-Major Malone, acting groom, valet, and butler), and had himself ushered into the drawing-room, where Dick and Nora were sitting by a cheerful fire.

Now, there was no reason why Scheiner should not call on them. He had often been there before, on good terms, had taken them out yachting, and, as far as he was 'officially' aware, they were as well-disposed to him as ever. If he suspected that the

machinations of that interfering person
Cunningham had to any extent alienated
their confidence in him, it was not for him
to show or admit to himself that he felt
any such suspicion. The truth was that
Scheiner had conceived a passionate admiration for Nora Scanlan, which was not quite
what is properly called love, as it consisted
wholly of a keen and sensitive appreciation
of her physical beauty, coexisting quite
naturally with an utter contempt for her
mental attainments and abilities. In consequence he ventured on such steps as the
present, in spite of their obvious rashness,
under his present peculiar circumstances.
As to the legitimacy of a married man entertaining and cultivating a sensuous inclination
for a most pure and blameless young lady,
such a course was evidently illicit ; but that
is a point which Leo Scheiner would
naturally ignore with perfect lightness of
heart.

' There is no punishment for such things,'
he would argue, ' except remorse, which is

easily cured by getting up an interest in a new lady. Plenty of them.'

So he greeted the Scanlans with his usual smiling politeness, inquired after their health, talked about foreign travelling, and behaved altogether in such an agreeable manner that the two good orphans began to wonder if it were possible for such a person ever to do any harm to anybody, and began to be a trifle ashamed of the rather cold manner in which they had at first received him. Why, what harm could there be in him? He sat there, talking with child-like gaiety in an easy, motiveless way, and nursing Miss Scanlan's black cat on his knees, and talking cat-talk to it, inducing it to walk round his shoulders, leaning forward with a laughing shriek when it tickled the back of his neck with its fur, and folding its tail round his neck. Oh, he was a nice man, and a good-looking one!

Having smoothed them down, and gained their favourable attention, much as he had the cat's, he shot out his sting in a moment, like a good fencer who has been amusing his inferior opponent, and biding his time.

'I think my friend Johnny Smalley told me Mr. Cunningham accompanied you on your Italian tour?'

Nora said nothing.

'He did,' replied Dick, 'and a very good chap he is to have with one. I don't know what we would have done without him at all.'

'Yes; a very clever man, and agreeable, I should suppose, though I do not know him intimately. What you would call a jolly fellow, I suppose?'

'Oh, he is. You wouldn't think so till you know him well, though. He takes a lot of knowing, and then you don't know him.'

'Like Hegel; a man who could keep a secret—for years—from everybody, for instance. I quite agree with you. Now, no one here would have imagined that marriage of his, had not accident revealed it.'

' What's that you say ?' said Nora, standing up before him like an offended goddess.

' I said his marriage,' replied Scheiner, in a tone of innocent and arch good-humour. ' I should be sorry to insinuate that it was any less—less legitimate relation. But have you not heard of it ? Perhaps I am indiscreet.'

' Sit down, now, Nora, and be quiet a minute. What is this, Scheiner ? I am after hearing this for the first time. Will you just explain to us now ?'

' It appears that there is a lady living in London, in Golden Square, passing by the name of Mrs. Denison, who is usually seen in the company of Mr. Cunningham, that there is a little boy at school, that Mr. Cunningham pays the tradesmen's bills, the doctor, the little boy's schooling, and so further. I assume it to be marriage, because I should regret to be so uncharitable as to assume otherwise.'

' Well,' said Dick, ' and me trusting him like a brother !'

'Ah!' said Scheiner, 'I was wrong.   I have given pain.   I should not have spoken.'

'It is no matter whether you spoke or not,' said Nora, 'I don't believe a word of it.   Mr. Cunningham is the master of his own actions, but I don't believe he ever spoke or acted a lie in his life.   Of course, it is no concern of mine.'

'Of course.   I am glad of that.'

'Then, you thought it was?   And that was why you brought the tale to me?'

This, a *riposte* as sudden and fierce as his own attack had been quick and cruel, made even Scheiner wince for a moment, but he replied :

'Such an action I could not understand. I happened to hear Mr. Cunningham himself talking about the matter quite openly with Dr. Hanlon, the new doctor, who, it appears, attended the Golden Square *ménage* at one time.   Others were present at the time— Mr. Paynter, for example—I thought you would know.   What Mr. Paynter knows is usually soon public property,' added Scheiner, with a smile.

Dick said nothing, but was plunged in thought.

Nora replied again :

' I don't believe it.   If you got the whole College of Physicians to swear it, and all the gossips of Redcliff to repeat it, and you swept purgatory of all the dirty liars in it, from Ananias to Pigott, to bear witness, I wouldn't believe it.   See that, now ?   And don't be talking to me about it again.'

And she left the room, to go upstairs and lie face downwards on her own bed in a wild passion of angry tears.   For she was afraid she did believe it.

Dick looked at Scheiner, and said, in an unnaturally calm voice :

' I think you had better clear out now. If you'll excuse me, I don't feel quite well.'

' All right, my dear fellow.   I quite understand.'

And Scheiner put on his fur coat and cap, and trudged home through the snow in the dark, humming 'Du bist wie eine Blume.'

When he got back to the Royal Riviera, he got ready for dinner in his own room, then came into the sitting-room, to find his wife sitting in an armchair reading a novel, and seemingly in a calm frame of mind. He pleasantly quoted Mother Hubbard.

'Where have you been?' said she.

'To the post, and then to the Club,' replied he, holding his hands out before the fire, and smiling at his face in the mirror.

'What a miserable liar you are! Why can't you say you have been to see that woman?'

'It is of no use to argue with you, but why should I say so?'

'Not a bit. I am beginning to know you. You couldn't tell the truth if you wanted to.'

'Considering the large profits which can be made by the contrary course, perhaps that is well. I am in a pleasant humour now, and you shall abuse me as much as you like, and I won't lose my temper. But it's all nonsense and waste of time. Do you think this young man of ours, this Johnny, can be brought to put in five thousand before his friend Cunningham comes back ?'

' I fancy he will part to a certain amount, any time you like to ask him. But he would perhaps give more in time, if he were not pressed. He doesn't just love the idea of selling the real estate, because he is sharp enough to know that all those ground-rents are a good security, although his fool of a mother does her best to help us, and his sisters to a less extent—at least, the two grown-up ones. The others are mere children, of course, and do not concern themselves with business.'

' High interest is what the women think of, of course. What will he do, say, to-morrow ?'

' Why be in such a hurry ? You will get more by waiting.'

' I have all the scrip, with coupons attached, ready, to any value required. Why am I in a hurry ? Because, as I told you already to-day, we cannot stay here much longer. Since I told you that, things have occurred which make that statement more true, and our time shorter.'

' What things have occurred ?'

' Never mind, at present. I shall perhaps do well to sacrifice a great deal for the sake of getting a little. I could work with freer hands, I think, if you would return to London and wait for me there. You could take most of my things in your trunks, so that, if I subsequently had to leave in a hurry, this den of thieves called a hotel would not have any baggage worth anything to steal, or detain, as they call it. It was a brilliant idea of mine to have the bill presented monthly. The manager was charmed, because it implied that we should make a prolonged stay. I almost wish I had made it quarterly. I think he would have accepted it, and it would have saved much inconvenience. If ever I can lower myself to the level of a common thief, I will keep a seaside hotel, adapted for wedded couples, American tourists, and foreign noblemen.'

'You want me to go to town again and wait for you?'

'Yes. I will get a cheque from Johnny for as much scrip and coupons as he will take, and go straight to town as soon as I have it. It will be some time before the hotel realizes that we are not coming back, and by that time we shall be across the Channel.'

'Leo, do you think I don't see through you? All this alarm and hurry is pure invention, and you simply want to get me out of the way for you to carry on with that woman. Perhaps you have made arrangements to run away with her, for all I know. Something must have happened to bring you home in such an improved temper.'

Leo lifted up his hands and made a grimace, the desperate, tired grimace of a man who has tried to make an obstinate, unreasonable woman see reason, and is driven to the utmost limit of his patience.

'Herrgott in Himmelskreuzsakkerment

und Donnerwetter und schock-Schwerernoth!
'Noch a' mal!   It is enough to make a man
become a grocer or a missionary!   To have
all the labour, expense, patience and intelligence of months made worthless, a beautiful scheme upset by a miserable fool of a
jealous woman!   Listen to me, you——
you overfed cat.   When I say that I do not
care if that Scanlan girl is at the bottom of
the sea at this moment, and that there is
real risk in delay—risk of policemen and
prison (partly through that illegitimate son
of a pig Cunningham), and that you are doing
your best to ruin me, and yourself too, it is
as seriously true as that I am a thief and
that you are a ——.   Let us put the dots
on the "i's" for once, as you have developed
such a desire to hear truths.'

Here the bell clanged through the house
for the *table d'hôte*, and the debate was
adjourned.   Mr. and Mrs. Scheiner unbent
at table, and were extremely agreeable to the
few fellow-guests who had been induced by
their doctors to winter at Redcliff.

CHAPTER XXVIII.

'THAT is not a bad idea of Kitty's.' Scheiner was meditating alone in a comfortable leather chair in the smoking-room of the hotel, where he had taken refuge after dinner to avoid further debate until he had had time to develop ideas, and to arrange in his own mind what had better next be done. 'That is a good idea. It is quite true that Miss Scanlan is the only woman in this place besides Kitty—"gentle Kate"—who is becoming ungentle and dangerous. Decidedly dangerous! She has done a good deal for me, nearly as much as I can expect to get out of her. It would be a pity to fail ridiculously because of such a woman's temper. We must not

VOL. III.   48

overdrive the willing horse ; we must turn
her out to grass, on the contrary, and
engage another one as soon as possible.
This other woman is full of noble emotions
and passionate impulses, a beautiful fool,
superstitious, ignorant, probably revengeful,
and rich. That is all good material, and it
would not be the first time if I were the
torch to kindle such inflammables, and into
most agreeable fireworks. There was a
time when I could wile away romantic
ladies from their quiet homes, I remember,
even as fowls are decoyed, lizards whistled
to, flies netted in webs, mice lured by
cheese, and pretty, shining, speckled and
valuable fish attracted by an ingenious
artificial insect with a hook in it. Yes,
and their papas and mammas and husbands
sometimes came down handsomely ; sometimes not. I am not old yet ; my hair is
not white, my waist is thin, and my tongue
is fluent. What has been can be. And
now is the moment to catch my damsel on
the rebound. She is proud, and very angry.

She believed every word of my story—why not? The story is true. Even I could not have invented a better. It was simply my Destiny which stepped out of its machine and helped me. My friend Cunningham has a *collage* in London, most naturally. Equally naturally, he does not make it a subject of conversation in Redcliff, where provincial views of such matters obtain. And then my Destiny comes in, in the form of a foolish little fat doctor, and I find it all out. I think I am nearly even with that unbeliever in Irredentism now. When he comes back here, his lady, with her pride and her temper, will not listen to any extemporized mystifications, and it will be difficult for him to extemporize anything which will explain the lady away, *and* account for the little boy. Then they will quarrel and separate, and the great *Brumm-ochse* of a brother will tell him they are not at home if he should call again, and perhaps break his head as well. Then I come in. So! I know my human nature ;

I could write a brilliant thesis on human nature. I am a very clever fellow. And gentle Kate? She thinks me ungrateful, and says she has worked for my interests *und so weiter*. Naturally. What would be the good of her if she did not work for me? If I keep a dog I expect him to fetch sticks out of the water, or pursue or indicate the presence of game, or pick out a named card. I think that it is she who is ungrateful. Kitty must be removed for a time, say a month or six weeks, to recover a proper sense of her position. She will be glad to come back on any terms after that, if I want her. I had better take her trunks and put them in the cloak-room at Waterloo, and keep the ticket. A woman's wardrobe is a valuable hostage. I shall do this before I escort her to town. I think a good strategist was lost in me. When I determine on a plan I carry it out promptly. She will go after her clothes as a cat after valerian, and I shall be free to act as my Destiny directs here. If I am driven to it, I leave, not otherwise, and not before I have floated the Casino again ; all these good people want money —Paynter, Moore, the Vicar, and the mad General who prophesies. He is converting me from the errors of Rome, and I flatter myself I shall " convert " a good deal of my floating exterior debt with his help. Then, I have promised the Vicar a new organ—a sumptuous organ—he shall have the monkey too, if he likes. Oh, I think these good people would not believe it, if policemen came and said nasty things about me. I almost think they would attempt a violent rescue. And I will be very much in love with Miss Scanlan, and perhaps the *Brumm-ochse* will become a vice-president, or take some Cretan Loan—the seven per cent. mortgage debentures guaranteed by Government for the purpose of constructing a railway through a country rich in mineral wealth. Issued at 9 5. I am certainly a very clever fellow.'

And he went upstairs and to bed, and

slept like an innocent boy with a placid face.

The next day Kitty Scheiner came into the sitting-room to breakfast, and Leo, who was waiting, said :

' I have explained in the hotel that you will go up to town this afternoon by a convenient train, that you are going to consult your physician. I explained to you yesterday all about it.'

' I shall not go.'

She spoke in an ominous, quiet contralto.

Leo sat down, and tucked in his napkin round his neck, like a pinafore.

' Very well. I shall, unfortunately, before long, and perhaps without warning. Do you wish to be left here alone, to pay the bill and explain things ?'

' Why do you want me to go so soon ?'

' I am like the captain of a ship, who in an emergency sees the passengers and crew safely off before he quits her himself.'

'I recognise you there. Heroism was your strong point every time.'

'Take some of these *œufs à la Bercy*, and help yourself to wine.'

Kitty sat down sulkily, and did not display much appetite. After a pause she said :

'I know as well as if you told me. It is written on your face that you want me out of the way—I suppose, to desert me altogether.'

'Nobody but a fool quarrels at breakfast. Take a glass of wine. There is plenty of time to make a row afterwards, if you must make a row. I wish you would keep up a more refined tone of conversation. You will forget yourself in public one of these days.'

Kitty drank some claret-and-seltzer and laughed, *hohl und grell*, and replied :

'You must take me as I am made. If you want a refined tone and all those things you've suddenly got so stuck on, you'd best go to Miss Scanlan. You don't want me to act the fool with you, as I do with poor Johnny Smalley, I suppose ?'

Leo, having just filled his mouth with a mixture of egg and sausage, made no intelligible reply. But he shook his head. She continued, in that queer mixture of colloquial American, spoken in a slight French accent, which was natural to her :

' I knew it from the first. I told you at the start that I would help, stand any racket you happened to be carrying on, on condition that you were square to me. And it is always the same. Underhand attempts to get at this woman, lies to me. It is ungrateful, but that is of no account, I suppose. It is treacherous. You mean me to get left—I know !'

' I am sick and tired of your jealousy, of the sight of your face and the sound of your silly tongue, and you may go to the everlasting misery if you cannot be pleasant,' replied Scheiner, irritated from his ordinary calmness by this persistent plaintiff.

'And leave you to her! I should think so! That's just what you want.'

'Very well. She is worth it. She is a woman with a better face, a better figure, better taste, better manners, than you, is several years younger than you, and has the additional advantage of lacking your origin and experiences.'

'Her origin is not one bit better than mine, I believe. And it's not for you to throw my experiences at me, of all people. I know I grew out of the mud of New York and Paris, and I suppose I shall go back to it again. My father was a wine-drummer, and my mother a singer in a Bowery Dive, and afterwards at a *beuglant* at the Boulevart Rochechouart, and he died in prison, where he was sent for killing her when he was drunk. I have always lived more or less on the cross, I suppose because it runs in the family, and we are built that way. And Paris and New York are both capital places for a young girl of my antecedents to make a living in. But whatever

I was, I never was a thief till you taught me.'

Here Kitty rose with some dignity from the table.

'Ah ! you underrate yourself, I am afraid.'

She turned suddenly round on him, and retorted :

'You ! What are you ? I have stuck to you through times bad and good, I have carried out all your orders, I have lied for you, stolen, blackmailed, flattered, cringed, tolerated the patronage and attentions of intoxicated young fools and abominable old men to get money and diamonds—all for you ! I am, I suppose, a decoy, a thief, a shameless woman, all through you, and for the sake of you, who want now to throw me over and get rid of me, that you may go and sponge on another, if she's as big a fool as I have been and the others. Yet I am better than you, for I have loved you as truly as any straight woman could, and would have died for you. After all, you are not worth it—you, who taunt me with my age after I have spent my best years in a sink of degradation for your sake. You are not worth lying for, much less dying for, you cowardly, selfish, dirty little German Jew !'

Leopold Scheiner drew the line at being called a German Jew, and he sprang up and struck Annie Stride in the face with his open hand, so that she staggered, being but a slenderly-made, frail woman.

'You dare to speak to me like that! You miserable street-walker, who had not one centime in the world, and owed money which I paid for you, when I picked you up ! I bought you body and soul—not that I want your soul !

'" Deine Seele kannst du begraben
    Hab' selber Seele genung."

I have fed you, clothed you, given you money to spend, and treated you in all ways like a lady. And you talk to me of ingratitude. *Pfui !* I spit on you !'

Kitty stood still in the middle of the room, with her arms hanging at her sides, her fists clenched, drawing long deep breaths which were almost sobs.   After a pause she said quietly, in her most monotonous, sing-song tone :

'I will kill you ! Take everything of mine you have not taken already.   I will go back to the streets and the prisons ; but I will kill you ! Don't you forget it. You are afraid of death ; I am not.   That will be something for you to look forward to.'

'I suppose you will betray me ?' said Scheiner, as it dawned on him what a fool he had been, and he recalled the fable of the goose with the golden eggs.

'Betray ?   No ! That's more in your line.   I shall not betray you ; but I shall kill you.'

'There, I suppose it is not difficult for each of us to remind the other of unpleasant things and undignified situations. What is the use ?   Let us make peace.'

'Peace! Now you are afraid, you see. You should have thought of that sooner.'

'Well, an armistice—a *Waffenstillstand*. I will begin by saying that I was so far carried away by a momentary emotion as to strike you. I would withdraw that if I could.'

'I believe I called you a selfish and cowardly little German Jew! I would withdraw that if I could,' replied she ironically.

A knock came at the door, and one of the waiters announced, 'Mr. Smalley!' and Johnny came in.

'Ah, good-morning! How are you all? It's turned out quite a decent day, and the snow's left off. I hear there is good skating to-day over at Lingwood. The creek has been kept flooded for some days past. I was wondering if all or any of you would like to come and try it?'

'You are kind — awfully kind!' said Scheiner; 'I think it would be delightful! My wife used to be a great skater on the

lake we used to have in Dalmatia. Kitty,
I think we have no engagements? No.
Then I will see Smalley eat some breakfast
here, and drink a glass of wine, while you
dress. Select a warm costume—I can trust
you to select a becoming one.'

And Leo laughed pleasantly as he patted
her on the shoulder. As she shook hands
with Johnny, felt the reluctance of his hands
to leave hers, and saw the sad, sincere light of
love in his eyes, she thought, ' He's a good
sort, poor boy! and would be ready and willing to spend all he was worth in trying to
make me happy. It is a shame!' Aloud
she said :

' Yes, you have some breakfast. There's
plenty on the table. I had not a good
appetite this morning. But I have no
skates.'

' That's easily remedied. The iron-
monger's windows are full of them, like the
blue things that grow up suddenly in the
shops in boat-race time. We'll go past

there, and I'll get you a pair—that is, if we can find any small enough.'

' Thank you.'

' Hullo ! what have you been doing to your face ? There is a pink mark on this side.'

Kitty smiled.

' Oh, Leo has been boxing my ears !' Johnny laughed incredulously. ' No ; in reality, I have been sitting with one side towards the fire, and got roasted. That will be all right when we go out. I will go and prepare myself. But I'm afraid I do not remember how to skate.'

' That will come all right. I'll see that you don't come to grief. Put on some lace-up boots—heels not quite so high as usual, if possible.'

' A vos ordres, milord. Serviteur !'

And she gave a bob curtsy, like the village little girls of Redcliff, as she left the room, and in an adjoining room they heard her whistling.

' Now sit down, my friend, and let me

give you something to drink. There will be a little dish, a nice little dish, for you in a few minutes—yes, a pretty kettle of fish. At least, eggs.' Then Leo went to his sideboard, and brought out a bottle and some more wineglasses. He proceeded to open the bottle and fill the glasses. 'Now, this wine is called Voeslauer, because it grows at Voeslau-bei-Wien, and it is suitable for a winter day, at breakfast-time. And we will make a little ceremony with it, with your leave, such as German students use when they establish and confirm a friendship, and say *Du* instead of *Sie* to one another. It is called drinking a *Schmolles*, and it is time you and I did it.'

'All right,' said Johnny amicably, but with the English shyness of sentiment and ceremony.

And the bright little man stood before him, glass in hand, hooked their arms across in the orthodox way, and they drank, and then Leo Scheiner gave Johnny's hand an honest, manly grasp, and said :

'Sei mein Freund, hierathe meine Schwester, besorge meine Kinder, bezahle meine Schulden !'

Scheiner purposely pronounced the words slowly and distinctly, so as to be comprehensible to the Ollendorffian mind. Johnny blushed, grinned, and said :

'Thanks, awfully. Queer old customs you keep up still !'

'Yes ; in Europe they live in an older world than you do in England. Competition and the rising tide of progress have not washed all their old sentimentalities, ceremonies and traditions quite away yet.'

Johnny looked round at the door. No, the lady was not ready yet. And a dish was brought him, and he ate, while Leo chattered pleasantly of many things, and saw that his young guest's glass was filled with the red Voeslauer Goldeck.

Johnny looked thinner in the face, more serious, if not anxious, and, in short, older than when we first saw him in the May sunshine in Birdcage Walk. Whether it was the cares of state, *i.e.*, of being head of a family and an owner of property, or whether he felt some painful suspicion that he was making a sad fool of himself, I cannot say —perhaps both—but something, at any rate, seemed to have 'taken it out of him,' and changed him from a boy into a man, though he still kept some semblance of the old boyish high spirits.

By the time he had finished eating and drinking, and accepted one of Leo's cigarettes, Kitty came in, in a fur cap and well-fitting seal jacket, and a dark-brown kilted skirt, a very pleasing figure. Indeed, Johnny thought she looked like a person in a picture, 'Portrait of Madame X——,' as the Salon catalogue puts it, and reflected with some satisfaction :

'Well, they can all say what they like, there's no other woman in or near Redcliff —except, perhaps, dear old Paddy—who knows how to wear clothes. I suppose that's why they are all jealous of her.'

Kitty approached the two men with that

slightly swinging gait of hers which can only be called swagger, but is not at all well described by that aggressive word.   It is done with facial expression, and poise of head, shoulders, heels, hips, skirt, everything ; it betokens satisfaction with self, and a desire to attract admiration, and it requires a critical sense of taste and a keen perception of the absurd not to overdo or caricature.   It can only be acquired in Paris, and square shoulders and high heels are recommended to the beginner, as well as clean smooth asphalte to practise on.

' Will these do ?' she said to Johnny.

Johnny looked in the required direction.

' Oh yes, they'll do.   You mustn't mind having holes gimbled for the heel-screws. We had better be going soon,' he added, looking at his watch ; ' there's a train at 1.20.'

So the three of them set forth, Johnny in a thick brown corded velvet jacket, breeches of the same, thick laced boots and knitted stockings, and a cloth cap ; Scheiner

in the fur coat and cap of which mention
has been made. Johnny swung a pair of
' Acmes ' in one hand and a stick in the
other, and round his waist, under his waist-
coat, hung a whole arsenal of metal things :
knives, gimlets, corkscrews, a folding foot-
rule, a watch, seals, a match-box, a folding
mirror like a locket, and a cigarette-case.
He looked symmetrical, picturesque, and
handsome—perhaps a trifle too much like
the heroes of stories as portrayed in Christmas numbers of illustrated serials ; but this
is hyper-criticism.

Lingwood was a small village about seven
miles from Redcliff, approachable by railway.
That is to say, there was a station bearing
the name of Lingwood, which was nearer to
the village of Lingwood than were other
stations bearing other names, on a line which
prided itself on being as remote as possible
from the places it was supposed to go to.
Lingwood proper was situated on both sides
of a creek, which was deep enough to float
a fair-sized row-boat at high water, and

corks and pieces of paper at low water. A stone bridge crossed the creek at Lingwood, and joined one side of the village to the other. A road went over the bridge and through the village. On the inland side of the bridge the creek expanded into a wide shallow mere, with flat meadows alongside it, and behind the meadows green downs with patches of wood up their sides, while a stream oozed along the bottom between the hills, shaded by tall trees and luxuriant underwood, through dark, lonely, and mysterious places, where the soil bore no footsteps long, being sucking, quivering mud, where the water had strange iridescent films, dull red tinges, and metallic sheen, or even sometimes looked as if a red snail had wandered over its surface. And the stream mingled sadly with the sea, and the upper creek was like a lake at high tide, like a mud-flat with wandering threads of water at ebb. The upper creek went pretty far up the country, until, in fact, it reached the foot of the downs, in the valley of which was the stream spoken of, and its uncanny overshadowed estuary ; and all the way from Lingwood Bridge up to the downs, on both sides of the creek, were growing wood, rushes, grass, and water, but never a human house.

It was a silent, beautiful place. It fascinated little children who went wandering on summer afternoons up the creek, in the flat meadows, while the sun made the water silver, until they got into the shade of the trees and hills, and saw the strange colours of the pools, and the queer glistening markings on the surface, and the busy leaping insects on the mud ; and then they got frightened, suddenly discovered that they were alone, thought things lurked there in ambush for them, joined hands, and ran away to the sunshine and safety of the village.

In the moonlight summer nights, sorcerers come and hold May meetings and June junketings up at the shady upper end of that creek. The young witch, the *Chovihani*, leaves the gipsy camp and sails in an egg-shell, which (as is well known to sorcerers), can be expanded into a beautiful, swift, and capacious barge, and floats about the upper creek with a corpse-candle. There are those who have seen the faint, flitting, unholy light, and among them one who says he knows that *Chovihani*, and that her name is Methane, and her initials CH_4^- ; but, then, some people know too much.

Furthermore, there was in the bridge at Lingwood a sluice-gate—in fact, two sluice-gates—and the use of them was to shut the water into the upper creek when the tide ebbed from the lower or sea side of the bridge. And the use of that was, that the water on the upper side might be let out through one gate only, afterwards, so as to work a mill which stood at one end of the bridge, leaving just room for the road to pass between it and the water. In the tunnel under the mill was a wheel, and under the wheel in the semi-darkness shot the roaring, frothing, splashing water, and ground flour until the upper creek was empty.

But now the upper creek was entirely shut off, and the mill did not go. The meadows, and the downs, and the trees, and the village house-tops were all assimilated, and their outlines softened, by snow, and the creek was a frozen lake, upon which merry skaters flew or fell, puzzled dogs overran the objects they pursued, and got involved in skaters' legs, so that the latter leapt, swore aloud, and tumbled crashingly, while the dog wailed with futile pawings of the ice, and village lads in red comforters and hobnailed boots shouted as they slid in long processions.

After the train had come in from Redcliff, a fresh batch of skaters of both sexes came pouring down the steep road into the village, formed along the banks below the road, put on skates, and advanced in extended order to reinforce the already numerous pleasure-seekers. Casualties fell

out, to continue the metaphor, with fre-
quency.

But Johnny and Mrs. Scheiner could
both skate, and they sped away together,
straight away for the far upper end, where
the dark valley began and the sunshine was
not, and the water ceased to be salt or fresh,
and the mud-witch and her daughters
brewed poison for the god of flies.

As they passed, a careful observer might
have noticed that people said things about
them. It is not to be supposed that the
movements and inclinations, real or imaginary,
of a young man just ' come into his property '
like Johnny, and of a brilliant but peculiar
personality like Mrs. Kitty Scheiner, were
let pass without comment. In Redcliff, the
gentry, tradesmen, and the servants formed
between them a very complete court of
inquiry or commission, reporting from time
to time. What they reported depended
mainly on their frame of mind, and whether
they were amiably disposed, or the contrary,
towards the subjects of the inquiry. Of all

that, however, Johnny was regardless, or ignorant. He was happy for the moment, and, like the songbirds of the poet, he 'recked of no eerie To-come.' Modern young men probably seldom do, especially when skating cross-handed with a nice woman with whom they are on 'most favoured nation' terms, or think they are.

'I did not see your cousins, Mr. and Miss Scanlan,' said she.

'No more did I.' As they left the circling crowd behind them, and shot out into the unexplored and solitary further stretches of the creek, Johnny said : 'Don't you think skating is something like life ? There are all the ordinary mindless pumps going round and round in the prescribed orbit, all alike, where they can all see one another, and all be desperately amused and pleased if one of them tumbles down or goes under ; and here we are, deliberately advancing into the unknown, perhaps the unsafe, and turning our backs as much as possible on convention.'

And the rising ground on the right flank began to hide the sun from them.

'Where did *you* learn to moralize?' replied she carelessly.

'I don't know. It struck me. Perhaps it is a little prosy, and not as entirely original as my ideas generally are.'

'I hope the ice is not dangerous where we are going.'

'Literally or metaphorically?'

'Both, if you insist. But literally, to begin with.'

'I don't see why it should be; but if it gives way, there is only some six or ten inches of water, and some greenish-gray mud underneath.'

'Br-r-r-r! It is not exactly cheerful here,' she said, as they became more and more enclosed in the valley, and the surface of ice became narrower.

After some little time, Johnny found her rather silent, and apparently thoughtful, and not as full of amusing subacid chatter as usual, and he asked her what was the matter. Of course she said 'Nothing.' Then, like every young man under similar circumstances, he thought it had something to do with himself, and asked if he had offended her in any way, to which she replied, 'Not at all—on the contrary.' Was it anything in which he could help her in any way? 'No. Oh no! Perhaps I am a little—out of sorts.'

Perhaps! Perhaps it was the chill gloom of the place where they were. Perhaps it had something to do with an old-fashioned thing called conscience. And perhaps it had not.

'I want to go back into the sunshine,' said she, after a pause.

'Well, if you like. Only it's so public there.'

'Not so very public. They can see, but they cannot hear.'

'Before we go, I want to tell you—you know, of course, what I think about you, lots that I mustn't tell you. I know,' Johnny continued incoherently, 'I'm not particularly clever, and I don't know all about foreign countries, and books, and society, and all that sort of thing, like you ; and my birth—well, my people have been honest sort of people mostly, though middle-class, don't you know ; but we don't claim to any particular rank or ancestry, so I don't profess to be particularly interesting. I believe my great-grandfather was a common sailor, and if he could write his own name he was probably proud of the accomplishment. But he was a good Englishman, and died for England with Nelson. Let that go. I've a pretty clean record, I think, as records go. And God knows, if I ever had the chance, I'd try to make you happy—you know that ?'

' I believe you would ! Johnny, you are a very good fellow—you don't know how much so.'

' Don't I ? I know I'm talking like a maundering idiot.'

' No. But, you know, I am much older than you, and I tell you all this is rubbish.'

' You older ?   What's three or four years ?   Why, I'm twenty-six this spring myself.'

' Ah ! you wait till you are thirty, then marry a nice, pretty girl of twenty-two, then you will say some day, " That poor Kitty Scheiner I used to flirt with must be quite old now, and ugly, with a wrinkled face, and tinted hair, and false teeth." That's what you will say, if it's only to please the nice girl.'

' It's nonsense to talk like that, and you know it.'

' What do you know about me, any way ? You don't know how I have spent my life, how many men I have—flirted with ; what my experiences have been ; what you call my record.'

' I don't know, and I don't care.   I know you as you are, and that is good enough for me.'

' You know me ?   Ah, Johnny !' and she smiled sadly again.   ' I do not think you do.   Say, what would your religious rela-

tions think if they heard this conversation ?'

' Oh, bother ! What do I care ?' Then,
in a different voice, he said, ' You like me,
don't you, Kitty ?'

She put one hand on his arm, and said
quietly and sadly, as they stood there on the
ice, in the gloom and solitude of the upper
creek, ' Yes, Johnny, I like you—not, perhaps, quite as much as you deserve to be
liked.'

He put his arms round her impulsively,
and kissed her, and the ice gave a loud
crack beneath them.

' Come away !' she said. ' I imagine we
are skating on pretty dangerous ice.'

And she laughed, and, taking his hands
again, they fled from that bewitched spot,
and back into sunshine and public view.

Immediately there advanced, with caution
but determination, Mr. Paynter. Mr.
Paynter could not skate, and did not.
Mrs. Paynter could not skate, and did.
But he was not to be balked of social

intercourse, and, having told everybody else on the ice what he had to tell, pounced (if a gingerly advance with short steps can be called 'pouncing') on Johnny and Mrs. Scheiner as a fresh prey.

'Hullo! I didn't see you before. Where have you been, eh? I say, have you heard? Cunningham's got a wife and family in London. I believe the Scanlans are awfully cut up about it, because she was sweet on him, rather, don't you know.'

'Really?' said Johnny. 'Well, I lived with him in London since we left the 'Varsity, until last summer, which he spent here, and I'll swear he hadn't then.'

'Oh, but there's no doubt about it. The new doctor, Hanlon — capital chap! — attended them.'

'Attended whom?'

'Oh, them. There's a little boy, you know.'

'Dr. Hanlon must have mixed up somebody else. This is the biggest bosh I ever heard, I assure you. I know Cunningham a great deal better than Dr. Hanlon, or you, either, and I tell you it's frantic, wild, impossible rot!'

'Oh, well, if you take it that way, it's no good telling you. But I thought, as you were an old friend of his, you'd like to hear he'd got into trouble.'

'Got married, you mean,' said Kitty Scheiner, coming to the rescue. And she and Johnny skated off at a pace Mr. Paynter could not attempt.

And the afternoon wore on, and the sun began to go down, dark yellow and red, beyond the snowy fields. Mr. Paynter managed to catch Kitty and Johnny once more, and said to the former:

'I say, Scheiner's off. He asked me to say he was going back to Redcliff, and that you were to follow at your convenience. You know he's a bit sweet, in a quiet way, on Miss Scanlan, and I expect he is going to take advantage of the opportunity, now the other gentleman's put into the shade.

Awfully improper, of course, but I shouldn't
be surprised.'

'No ?' said Kitty. 'You are a singularly
clever man, Mr. Paynter.' Then she added
to Johnny: 'I am quite tired. Will you
take my skates off and take me home ?'

He looked at her face in the fading light,
and saw a wild, weary look in her eyes.

'Yes. Come along. I think you've had
about enough of all this.'

'I think I have, nearly.'

As they went back in the train, their
compartment was full of chattering Redcliffites, and Kitty Scheiner spoke hardly a
word, but stared before her at the framed
advertisements of seaside hotels on the panel
of the first-class carriage. And the darkness came on.

When she got to the hotel she dismissed
Johnny, saying she was going to lie down
and go to sleep. Having got rid of him,
she went upstairs. No signs of Leo. She
settled in her mind, without asking anyone
a question, where he had gone, when he

slunk off from Lingwood Creek. And she
walked up and down, up and down, like a
leopard, in the sitting-room, working herself
into a desperate rage, and resolving what
was to be done. It was evening now, and
the moon had risen, and she looked out of
the window and saw it shining over the sea
and the snow-covered land. Then she went
on walking up and down, and all that Leo
had said and done that day passed before
her mind over and over again. Not a word
or deed had she forgotten. She poured out
a little glass of brandy and drank it, and
went on walking up and down in that
dreadful, restless, prowling way. She did
not pause at the looking-glasses as usual,
and she had not taken her outdoor things
off. She took one more little glass of
brandy, and all her savage pain, anger, and
jealousy ran in quicker, wilder, intensified
pulsations. She became the personification
of Malice Aforethought.

Then her mind became unnaturally quick
and imaginative. She looked round the

room rapidly, and seemed not to see what she wanted. Then she suddenly pulled a drawer of the sideboard open, looked in, and pushed it back with an impatient slam. She opened the other, took something out, put it in her muff, where it lay lengthways, projecting, certainly, but not conspicuous in mere moonlight, and then she went out for a walk. No one saw her go, and she made no noise, and met no one. She walked deliberately along the road, her heels punching little round holes in the snow. Whether she had any purpose or not in going in that direction, she looked as if she had. In time she arrived at that part of the road where was the entrance-gate to the short gravel drive approaching The Oaks, where the Scanlans lived. She went in at that gate, on to the silent moonlit, snow-covered lawn which lay alongside the gravel approach, and looked at the windows. The drawing-room windows showed a light, but the blinds were down. The dining-room windows were evidently curtained, as the light only

appeared faintly at the edges. She saw
nothing, but heard a subdued murmur of
voices. She was as perfectly certain that
Leo was there as if she had seen him.

'Very well,' she decided ; 'I shall wait
for him.' And she waited, walking about in
the snow for quite two hours. It was
freezing hard, but she felt quite warm. Her
skin especially felt hot. She took snow and
rubbed her face with it once, but that made
the glow worse, and she thought what an
unusual complexion she must have just then.
After the lapse of time mentioned, she saw
a figure against the light at the drawing-
room blinds. She retreated into the shadow
of a cypress, near the gate. The figure
looked out. She thought : 'That is the
woman.' Another figure appeared. 'That
will be the man.'

The two figures, after a time, appeared to
become one figure, and she took hold of
what lay in her muff, and waited. *Elle
voyait rouge.*

Then the front-door opened, and a man

ran down the steps and walked rapidly along the frosty gravel path. His collar was up, and in the shade of the cypress and other shrubs near the gate the moonlight did not show his features, except a momentary glimpse of black hair and moustache ; but she had no doubt who the man was. She said nothing, but held her knife firmly, and drove it with all her power into his side, as he passed. He said something, and soon fell down, clear of the shadow on the lawn, and the moonlight fell upon his face ; but she did not stop to look at anything or listen to anything. She ran in deadly terror, now the deed was done, and all her desperate, half-intoxicated excitement went like the fire of a match dropped into water. She ran till she was out of breath, then walked as fast as she could, till she came to a part of the road quite near the cliff, on her way home. She went to the edge, and listened to the tide washing with its dull, rhythmic roar below. Then she looked round and behind her, saw no one, and flung the knife

as far as she could out seaward. Then she
knelt near the edge, and held her head over
to look, and saw that the sea came right up
to the cliff and broke against it. Then she
went back to the hotel and walked upstairs.
It struck her that she would have to account
for the time, and explain at the hotel why
she had not dined. Surely any story would
do for that. Mr. Scheiner had had to take
an evening train to town, and she had seen
him off, and she would order something
now.

She went first to her bedroom, lit the
gas, and examined herself. No blood ; at
least, none that she could see. She took
off her fur cap and jacket, changed her
boots, and washed her hands. When she
looked in the glass to tidy her hair, she
was surprised to see how very much as
usual her face looked. Then she went into
the sitting-room, and there saw, calmly
reading the newspaper, Leo. She stood,
blankly staring.

'Had a nice time ?' he said, looking up.

She fell into his arms, and clung to him, and said :

' Oh, Leo, Leo, Leo ! Take care of me now and always. Forgive all the foolish things I said to you. I'm your property, as you said, body and soul—yours and the devil's for ever—and I shall not struggle against it any more.'

Leo looked surprised, but said mildly :

' Very good ; I am extremely glad. Take a *petit verre.*' And he poured it out. She drank it, and it calmed her, and saved her probably from hysterics.

He whistled ' La donna e mobile ' softly. Then he said :

' You seem excited ?'

' Oh no ! It's all right now. Have you dined ?'

' Yes. I've been dining with Johnny at the Club. The money business is to be settled to-morrow, and all is well. You go to-morrow.'

' Yes, yes ! I will go as soon as you like.'

' And I must follow as soon as possible with the money, the cash—the oof, as Johnny pleasantly calls it. We will drink his health in Cliquot this evening, this last evening of our most successful, but far from exciting, residence in Redcliff, and next week, or thereabouts, our last month's bill will come due, and the Royal, the Imperial, the Immense Riviera Hotel will whistle for it, and we shall be where there is not so much snow and so much " proper," and where there is no Paynter.'

' What have you been doing ?'

(' No one saw me,' she thought, 'and the knife is gone. It is all safe. I wonder who it was ?')

' I got cold and tired at the skating, so I came back, and finding a warm fire at the Club, I sat before it till I went to sleep. Then your Johnny came, and was very amiable, and in course of time we dined, I delicately introducing a little business.'

' And now we will have some Cliquot *sec*. Yes ?'

'We will. There, I think you deserve some, after all the fatiguing and exciting things you have done to-day.'

She laughed.

CHAPTER XXIX.

Nora Scanlan did not sleep much the night after Mr. Scheiner's visit. During the evening Dick tried to induce her to discuss the story told by Scheiner, but she obstinately refused, and repeated : ' I've told you I don't believe it, and I don't want to talk about it.' So Dick thought it over by himself, and came to the conclusion that, as Cunningham would be down at Redcliff himself very soon, the best thing to do would be to quietly and straightforwardly tell him the whole matter, and ask him what explanation he had to give, which shows that Dick was not quite such a fool as Leo Scheiner had set him down.

But then Dick was not in love with

the accused person, which makes a great difference to the point of view, while Nora was. And it is a strange thing, but often found true, that people are more suspicious, with a suspicion quite cunning and imaginative, of those they love than of others whose conduct is comparatively indifferent to them. Wherefore Nora waked a winter night for sorrow and anger and contradictory thoughts about this man whom she loved and had dizened in her mental picture of him with all kinds of chivalrous qualities and noble aims, for whose actions she had constructed a transcendent standard which should place him on that solitary eminence among other humanity upon which a passionate and idealistic woman desires the man she loves to stand. She had looked on his intellect, his character, his physical person, and his whole self, as the satisfaction of a fastidious and exacting taste, and had formed opinions and expectations of him of which he never dreamed, and would have laughingly looked on as beyond his deserts

or capacities had he known them. And now?
Now she was asked to picture him the hero
of a commonplace intrigue. A woman,
in London, with a false name. Whether
married or not mattered little. The secrecy,
the deception, the moral and æsthetic plati-
tude of it all, were paltry, sordid, repulsive in
either case. How could he do it?

Then she began to try and imagine what
the woman was like, whether he had perhaps
taken her abroad once—perhaps to Venice,
too; no, that thought must not be pursued.
You see, Nora was a woman in years, but
not in experience of the ways of the world,
and things shocked her sensitive taste which
some women would hold as trivial. She
held yet by the innocent, almost childish,
notions of conduct in which she had been
brought up, an austere code which was
absurdly incompatible with many an accepted practice, many a condoned peccadillo
of modern society! She knew nothing
whatever of Ethics, and believed in many
a grotesque and pathetic superstition, and

was guided by feeling much more than by reason.

And she had a horror of a breach of faith or deception, because it was a sin against God and man, and not because truth has been generally held from experience and on *a priori* grounds to be expedient for the welfare of society and the individual. She held that truth should be told even when it was not obviously beneficial to the individual teller. In short, she did not regard honesty in the light of a policy at all, good, bad, or indifferent. Wherefore, what filled her with sorrow and shame—shame for him, not for herself—was the horrible treachery involved in this matter. It was exactly the same whether the relation with this woman was one recognised by the law or not. That was beside the question.

The thing was that both she, and presumably this other woman, had been treated falsely, and that by the man she had secretly set up as a model of honour and manly virtue, and invested with all the splendid and absurd attributes which an ignorant, sensitive, richly imaginative girl's mind, fed on simple old-world teachings, romances, and legends, would naturally invent.

When she came to London to be in a situation, she learned many things of which she had not previously known the existence, and some of the more obvious flaws in our social system did not fail to become apparent to her in the course of time, and her companions in the business explained to her the nature of some of them, of which she had never dreamed, and filled her mind with surprise and horror. She wondered how they could treat these things as subjects to joke about. Subsequently these matters were brought more immediately under her notice, taking the form of a grievous misfortune to one of her girl-comrades, who was callously betrayed and deserted by a man in the usual way—just the commonplace, deadly vulgar story we all know, with its usual concomitants—and Nora was stricken with

wrath, amazement, and compassion beyond
verbal expression, though capable of expression in facts. Must Cunningham, her
lover, her 'chummy,' whom she thought
so different to all other men, be compared
to *that* other man ? Oh, it could not be
true ! She had said she did not believe
it. She would not believe it. It was in-
sulting to him to believe it. And yet
there the miserable thing was, with names,
and addresses, and circumstantial details.
And so she spent the worst night of all
her life.

The morning following Cunningham came
down to Redcliff in the fast train from town
in good spirits, and on the whole well
pleased with himself, though remorseful about
Mrs. Denison, whom he had had to make
understand, 'without unnecessary violence,'
that his affections were distributed else-
where. He had done it as kindly, delicately,
and indirectly as he could, and after all,
poor fellow ! he had not only never meant
anything but kindness to her, but also had

never said or done anything in any way
recalling the manners and customs of the
common self-seeking 'masher.' Yet he felt
that he had somehow done a wrong and
cruel thing, and was very sorry that the
possibility of it had never dawned on him
at an earlier date. Outside, the snow fell
at intervals, and the sky was dark gray and
low; with yellowish openings and purple
thickenings in the slowly-moving clouds.
On arriving at Redcliff, Cunningham walked
first to the Rectory, where he deposited his
bag, had some conversation with his uncle,
and remained to lunch. After that he went
towards Fernbank, and before he reached
that house was met by Jane, who shook
hands with him cordially, and said :

'Oh, I'm so glad you've come back !
The plot's thickening.'

'It hasn't got any thicker, I hope, than
it was when I went to town ?'

'Well, it has, so far that Johnny has
actually made an appointment with that
man this week to give him a lot of

money, and take shares in this Casino Company for it. He's going to sign an agreement of some kind to sell some of his property over at Portsmouth and take this scrip, or whatever you call it, and the more you tell him not, the more he'll want to do it, I'm afraid. Besides, the others are all backing him up and snub me, and tell me I can't possibly know anything about business matters if I interfere ; and of course I can't reply that I *do*, or that Florrie has been " shadowing " them under my orders whenever they have business interviews in the library. That woman is said to be seedy, and going up to town to-day or to-morrow to see her physician. Johnny has gone to see her, I suppose. At any rate, he hasn't been in to lunch, and hasn't come in yet.'

' I'm sorry for that. I thought I should see him. Last time I talked to him I had not so much ground to stand on as I have now. I should have preferred to talk to him quietly and privately, as he won't like what I have to say. However, if this is to come off this week, I must stop it at any price, whether the method hurts his feelings or not. Perhaps it will do him good to be shaken up a bit, after all this foolishness and botheration.'

' It's awfully nice of you to take all this trouble,' said Jane, rather tearfully. ' I've nobody but you and the Scanlans to comfort me; and I'm only a girl, and Florrie's a mere child. You've no idea how horrid the whole thing has been.'

' Oh yes, I have. And I think the way you have behaved throughout does great credit both to your brains and pluck.'

' Now, do tell me what you have done. Have you been seeing detectives ?'

' Well, I've been doing a little of that sort of thing on my own account. But I'll tell you all about it by-and-bye. I've something else to do now.'

' In a hurry to get to The Oaks, I suppose ?'

'Now, I call that cheek! Moreover, I happen to be going at present in precisely the opposite direction. I am going up Romer Down.'

'In all that snow?'

'In part of it, at any rate. I'm going to see the aged recluse whose name is Barton.'

'Is *he* in it, too?'

'He's in it to this extent, if not more, that he has an interest in not being evicted from his dwelling, and consequently objects to the Casino Company; but he also knows other interesting things, at present confidential, because I don't want yon little alien, the intelligent foreigner, you know, to get any warning that anything is up.'

'I shall be as silent as the grave, you may rely on that; silenter, because the grave yawns sometimes. Then, you really think that he—S., you know—is a double-dyed criminal — a regular wrong un, as Johnny would say (if he only would)?'

'I more than think it. I haven't the smallest doubt about it.'

'This *is* Gaboriau, isn't it? I never hoped to live to be really in a plot like this.'

'Well, you'll have to jam it all into that novel of yours. Good-bye for the present.'

Then Cunningham went on a weary, chilly, and damp tramp up the down, where he had a long interview with the old mariner. When he came down again it had left off snowing, and the ground was thickly covered. He thought to himself: 'Now I have done all the business which is immediately possible I'll walk over and see Nora.'

And he went to The Oaks. Sergeant-Major Malone took his snowy wet ulster, just as he had taken another's fur coat yesterday, and showed him into the drawing-room, where he found Dick alone, standing about, and looking solemn and extremely uncomfortable. Cunningham advanced with his hand out, saying :

'Hallo, old chap ! Nice climate, isn't it ?'

Dick did not respond to the handshake,

and looked so particularly dismal that
Cunningham said :

' What is it, Dick ?   Anything the matter
with Nora ?'

' She's very well—never better.'

' Then, what the devil *is* the matter ?'

' Well, then, to tell the truth, Mrs. Denison is the matter.'

' Mrs. Denison !   How did you hear of
her ?   Hanlon, I suppose ?   Why, that's
the very person I've come to talk to you
about ; but that's no reason for adopting a
funereal manner, that I can see.'

' Look here, Cunningham, I've treated
you like a friend, and I've trusted you like
a brother, in every sense of the word ; and
I've got to ask you now, between man and
man, what this business is about Mrs.
Denison, and, for reasons you know of, I've
the right to ask you that.'

' Right !   Of course you have.   But
what is it you've got into your head about
it ?   Why the portentous gloom ?   Forgive me, I don't want to be offensive, and

you evidently feel seriously about it, but what *is* it ?'

' I'm told you're married to this woman, or nearly as bad.'

' Oh ! A light begins to break. You were told that, were you ? And who took the trouble and responsibility of telling you that ?'

' The little—well, Scheiner, if you must know. I suppose you have a right to be told that,' replied Dick, uneasy and ' bedevilled,' as he explained afterwards.

' He did, did he ? By the sword of my father, I'll give him his kail through the reek for that ! And you believed him ? Believed that I could be such an all-round bounder and infernal skunk as is implied in such a proposition ?'

' Honestly, I didn't know what to think. Ye see, I know what men are, and Nora, poor girl ! doesn't, no more than a baby. And I'll tell you she didn't believe it, and she told him she didn't believe it. I thought she'd have had the fellow's blood.'

' I am glad of that, at least. She in her innocence did me more justice than you in your supposed knowledge of the world. Anything more ?'

' There was a little boy mentioned. Not to speak of a doctor.'

' I see. I am represented to be the parent of the little boy. Nothing like realism and plenty of circumstantial detail, however trivial. Now then, you listen to me, Dick Scanlan, and I'll tell you the exact facts as briefly as possible. You will recollect one day last summer meeting me at the Academy ?'

' I do.'

' After that, I met you again at the restaurant, where I told you I picked up a little boy from a cab accident, and took him home, and explained to you that that had delayed me from keeping an appointment at the Law Courts ?'

' You did.'

' That little boy was Mrs. Denison's little boy, and that was the first time I ever saw

him in my life, and the first time I ever saw
his mother. Dr. Hanlon and the house
people can corroborate that, to a certain
extent, and it would not be difficult to prove
that that was the first time I had ever seen
her in the house or neighbourhood. She
was a poor woman, not clever, energetic, or
capable, who had met with undeserved
misfortune, and her child was running to
ruin in the gutters. She confided her affairs
to me, quite uninvited, and I was sorry for
her. She had suffered much, and hadn't a
friend in the world, and I helped her and
gave her advice, such as it was, and, actuated
by some impulse or other I can't explain, I
put the little boy to school, at a sort of
Kindergarten place kept by an old college
friend of mine, a clergyman of the English
Church, who is married, and beyond suspicion, and can corroborate so far as he is
concerned. I never spoke a word to her
which could be construed as love-making,
and I sometimes found her rather a nuisance
than otherwise. And as far as I know, or

can form an opinion, the life she leads is as
straight as the Bank. The new doctor here
said something to me the other day at the
Club, in that miserable little fraud's hearing, out of which the latter constructed all
this neat and plausible story, simply and
solely for the purpose of alienating you from
me, and doing me a bad turn. I told you
long ago he had his knife in me, principally
because I think him a conceited humbug,
and he knows it. Mrs. Denison's real name
is Mrs. Pellegrini, and I have just found
out now that Alessandro Pellegrini, her
husband, who deserted her, and really is the
father of the little boy Alexander, is a man
who has been probably married more than
once, and is just at present Mr. Leopold
Scheiner. He doesn't yet know who Mrs.
Denison really is. I identified him from a
photo in Mrs. D.'s possession, and from other
evidence of a circumstantial nature, not
worth detailing. Who the woman he
calls his wife is I don't know and don't
care ; but she is, of course, in the swim with

Scheiner ; moreover, Mrs. D. has her certifi-
cates of marriage and baptism of Alexander.
Is that plain ?'

Dick made an impatient gesture :

' Great heavens, man, I believe you !
And I beg your pardon for being such a
fool as to doubt you.'

And Dick shook hands and regained his
usual placidity.   Then he rang the bell.

' Sergeant-Major Malone.'

' Sir.'

' Will you let Miss Scanlan know I am
waiting to see her down here ?'

' I will, sir.'

When Nora came in, looking utterly tired
out, Dick said to her :

' It's all right.   We've been making
terrible fools of ourselves.   He'll tell you
all about it.'

And Dick left the room for awhile.
Whereupon Cunningham :

' I am glad you didn't believe what that
miserable little thing said about me.   Very
ingenious fable, too, as you will see.'

'Oh, chummy, I didn't believe it a bit, but it made me so miserable.'

''M.   Well, come here, and I'll tell you all about it.'

*   *   *   *   *

'You'll stay to dinner?'

'Yes—oh yes, I think I'll stay to dinner.'

CHAPTER XXX.

DURING dinner, which, with a blazing fire, a
shaded lamp, drawn curtains, and a glass or
two of good wine, helped our three friends
(of whom two were something more than
friends to one another) to forget the winter
wind, the bitter sky, and man's ingratitude,
Cunningham told what he had to tell about
Leopold Scheiner Pellegrini.

' It would take a book to tell the catalogue
of his offences, and a very entertaining book
it would probably be, when you come to
think of the ladies he has played duets
with, and paid attentions to here, the clergy
who have asked him to sing ballads and
play the fiddle, or whatever it is he does
play, at parochial entertainments, the Dorcas

societies he has read the poets aloud to, and the tradesmen who have alternately rushed him and trusted him. There's a good time coming for them all, I think, when they find out that he is a penniless, pushing, shallow swindler, whose origin is apparently Teuto-Semitic, whose only recommendation is his intimacy with a shady nobleman who haunts bucket-shops and third-rate gambling clubs. I am not sorry for them, to tell you the truth—except, of course, in poor Johnny's case—because they have mostly made up to him for what they thought they could get out of him. Redcliff, as a whole, contains so many insufferable, gabbling, rotten fools and inflated petty humbugs that I should find it in my heart to forgive Scheiner for giving them away. In fact, I should have let him have a quiet hint to disappear, if his recent behaviour towards me had not re-moved any lurking temptation to distemper justice with mercy.'

'He must be a clever little beggar,' said Dick ; 'he took me in entirely.'

Cunningham smiled dryly.

'Oh, he is clever enough. He is a Doctor Phil., of the distinguished University of Marburg, or professes to be, and I dare say it is true. He edited a newspaper once for some time, and some of his relatives occupy good, that is, respectable, commercial positions in New York and in Stuttgart. You see, I've been busy getting up his record. He has not the genius, nor, I fancy, the courage, to be a really successful swindler on a large scale. He is a petty little fraud, who gets up a little scaffolding round the foundations of a little plot, then he overloads it with self-conceit and jabber, until the whole fabric collapses and he runs away and hides. Yet he has a singular talent for living in comfort at other people's expense, and keeping on the windward side of the law. Of course he is sharp, has plenty of tact, and a fair superficial knowledge of human nature.'

'He knows a powerful lot of languages,' said Dick.

'Well, yes; fluent, and frequently incorrect, and totally devoid of any literary
knowledge; but he knows how to make the
utmost possible display of such talents as he
has. As to his principle of life, it may be
regarded as an absolutely cynical egoism,
destitute of any kind of scruple, sentiment,
or remorse, hidden under a thin surface of
apparent kindly good-humour and ready
mirth, and restrained only by extreme
personal cowardice. His stock-in-trade consists of impudence, some showy accomplishments, agreeable manners and appearance,
and a sort of officious omniscience. If
you want your scullery whitewashed, he
will know of a new, special sort of whitewash, destined to replace all hitherto
known kinds, accessible only to him, and
will probably add, in due course, that
there are " thousands in it," and try to
persuade you to take shares. Perhaps
you have met with that sort of thing,
Dick?'

'Indeed he did!' said Nora. 'He made

Dick take some shares in a new paper-clip which won't clip.'

' There you are, you see.'

' Ah, well, it wasn't much he had from me. And if I never see the money again, the poor little devil's welcome to it, for he's very amusing.'

' And how many more kind - hearted people have probably felt just the same, do you think ? That is a good case in point. Then, of course, he never pays anything he owes, unless he is absolutely compelled to. It is more petty sponging than actual robbery. The man who sold a whole theatre-full of tickets for a series of performances by Sarah Bernhardt, in a South American town which Sarah Bernhardt had no inten- tion of visiting, and was off in a steamer with a new name and an ingenious disguise long before they had spotted the fraud, was a hero compared to Mr. Scheiner.'

' And him saying he was a Catholic too !' said Nora.

' That's like Irredentism — a kind of

vague idea of distinction, don't you know.'

' It's my notion,' said Dick, ' that he'll bilk you yet. He knows too much.'

' He doesn't know much. He doesn't know who Mrs. Denison is, or he'd sooner have touched hot coals than meddled with that subject. It doesn't matter whether it's bigamy or not, because, either way, it ostracises him at Redcliff, you see. And as far as I understand from Mr. Satterthwaite, who has gone very thoroughly into the matter, and understands the technicalities of such things, he has made himself amenable to the law in the matter of this precious Casino. His friend, the Earl of Croagh-patrick, who has acted throughout the part of decoy—been a kind of mask for Scheiner to grin through—probably knows that, for he has left the country, presumably with his pockets well lined.'

' But supposing they really carried out this Casino business ?' said Dick.

' They won't ; and it would be a dead

failure if they did. It's not suited to the spirit and character of the place in the least, and would be managed in a way which would ensure bankruptcy, and then remain, a melancholy ruin, to be pointed out and described to strangers for years after as Redcliff's Folly, till some contractor bought up the materials and pulled it down ; and he would probably go bankrupt too before he had finished.'

' Faith, if you put it all in a book people wouldn't believe it.'

' Probably not. Or if a reviewer a trifle sharper than the average guessed that it was all too improbable not to have happened, he would trot out the useful maxim that it was with apparent not real truth that a novel-writer ought to deal, which, translated, means that things ought only to be described which the average mind might be led by the average experience to expect to happen.'

' Well, I should think there was only one kind of truth; but I don't know much about making up stories. All my stories are things I remember happening—funny things too, some of them,' observed Dick.

'Of course there is only one kind of truth, the kind you know by experience, and no other. Anything outside that is conjecture. And imagination is the quality which, with the aid of memory, joins up fragments of experience into nice kaleido-scopic patterns, and so constructs more or less fresh presentments of the same old facts.'

'But do you mean that nobody ever imagines anything which isn't made up of something he remembers?' asked Nora. 'How do you account for the fairy-tales? Because I suppose you are a deal too clever to believe them.'

'I mean that imagination, or "making up," never achieves something which hasn't got its original source in experience, however re-arranged and muddled up, just as you can construct or dissolve material objects in various ways, without being able to add to or take from the original matter of which they were made. Take your fairy-tales. When they are not mere misinterpretations of words which formerly meant something quite different, they are simply ordinary bits of experience stuck together in a new and pretty way something like dreams or parables. Just you try, now, to imagine something beyond your experience.'

Nora looked thoughtful.

' Well, then, heaven,' she suggested.

' All right. The word is one you have heard often enough, of course, but what idea do you attach to it ?'

' A world where people will be happy, and good, and where they won't be ill or die. And——'

' That will do, to begin with. Now, then —a world, happiness and goodness, illness and death. Surely those, or their contraries, are very ordinary forms of human experience? Your immortality is only the negation of the most universal experience mankind possesses. I don't count a negation as a new imaginative

creation. Besides, I'll throw in all the other
accompaniments too, if you like, harps,
crowns, wings, music, jewellery—all the
Oriental details—and you will find they are
simply human ordinary things put in un-
familiar relation occasionally, enlarged, multi-
plied, or turned upside down. Same with
other mythologies. But with regard to
telling stories, the fiction you make up ought,
I take it, to be as like the truth as you can
make it. And the likest way is for it to *be*
the truth, dressed with your artistic skill and
style into a fiction, even as the raw lobster,
eggs, cream, olives, lettuces, etc., of nature, are
dressed with skill and style into the mayon-
naise of art. The boshiest story-books of
to-day are the ones not " founded on fact,"
and belong to two kinds : those which echo,
repeat, and copy other books, and those
depending for their interest on miracles, *i.e.*,
negations of experience—ghosts, theosophy,
and all that.'

' I like them,' said Nora. 'But, then, I'm
not clever.'

'All right. But I still think that a conscientious imagination, which won't condescend to copy the phrases which come floating along the eddies of memory from other people's books, or to get cheap effects out of supernatural occurrences, or to take a " situation," and then work back and see how some unhappy marionettes may be driven up to that situation and pushed out of it again by a process called " construction," will found fiction on fact. And fact means experience. The personal and private experience is likely to be done best. The multiplication table contains a number of facts of universal experience, but they would only be of subordinate interest in a novel; while the private personal experience of a long, sallow, and truculent-looking Common Law barrister who fell hopelessly in love with an Irish lady of indescribable charms and uncertain temper would be far otherwise, I have no doubt.'

'Get away with that, now. But do you mean that an author has to go through all he writes about?'

' I don't mean that Shakespeare smothered his wife, poured hebenon into his brother's ear, or necessarily made a number of brutal remarks to a young lady, ending with a recommendation to adopt a conventual life ; but I do very much mean that he knew what jealousy was, what remorse was, what it was to be mad nor'-nor'-west, and surrounded by paltry falsities and powerful sins, and to meditate on that sleep wherein we say we end the heartache. Those are the real big facts. Whether he happened to know of a case of a man really killing his wife with a pillow, that the man was black, and (like other men since) was in love with a lady at Venice, is of very little consequence. But you don't make people feel things you haven't felt, or see things you don't already see.'

' Thank you, teacher,' said Nora.

' That Scheiner's got a lovely experience to draw from, I'll go bail,' said Dick.

' No doubt. By the way, I want to go round this evening, and see if I can

catch Johnny alone, and clear things up a
bit. I'd like to do it quietly, but if I can't
I'll just go to-morrow morning and do it
before his family, and Scheiner, and every-
one who may be there. It will be too late
then for delicacy and hesitation. But, you
see, the boy is a friend of mine of many
years' standing, and he's more a victim than
an offender in this unhappy attachment of
his, and I don't want to be instrumental in
making him ridiculous. It will be pretty
bad for him, any way, but I shouldn't like
to make it worse than I could help. I dare
say you understand. So, if you'll allow me,
I'll just smoke a cigar of Dick's, and then
go off to Fernbank and see the lie of the
land. After that I think I'll go round to
the Rectory, as it will be getting late.'

' I see,' said Nora ; ' and I think you are
right. Besides, the sooner you tell Johnny
all you know, the better. You did talk to
him before, didn't you ?'

' Yes, directly after we came back from
abroad ; but then I had not enough evi-

dence. Even now I've nothing definite against the woman, except that she is with the man. Poor Johnny didn't like it, you know, and called me names, and was generally intractable. Moreover, he said that if she turned out a beggar, and Scheiner an impostor, that didn't change his views of her personally, and so on. Very ominous endings, these! But if the man is nailed, you may be sure the woman will bolt.'

'How *can* he like her?' said Nora.

'That's a question that has been asked about so many people. How is it that really good, and perhaps clever, people are victimized by such very inferior people of the other sex so often?'

After a little while longer, Cunningham said 'Good-night,' and got up to go away, and went into the hall to put his coat on. Nora followed, and Dick stayed in the dining-room and smoked and smiled. In the hall Sergeant-Major Malone was doing something with a tray, so Nora, with rather more stateliness than usual, went into the

drawing-room, as if she had never entertained the idea for a moment of stopping in
the passage to take a private farewell of
anybody.

Cunningham, who perceived all this, and
was amused, went into the drawing-room,
ulster and all, and shut the door after him.
The lamp had been brought in, and the fire
made up. The curtains were not drawn,
and Nora was standing at the window,
holding the blind a little on one side. She
turned when Cunningham came in, and
said :

' Well, what do you want ? I thought
you were gone !' But her expression belied
her words.

' What were you looking at ?'

' I looked out to see if it's snowing. But
it isn't. It's a lovely night. Moonlight
above and snow below.'

' That's all right,' replied he, coming
nearer to the window. ' Now, I want you
to tell me : are you sure you are satisfied
about the truth of this story, as I told

it you, about that woman in Golden Square?'

Nora looked at him gravely, but quite candidly:

'Yes. Quite sure.'

'But you did believe the other story really, didn't you?'

'I won't tell you a lie. I partly believed it, and partly didn't know what to think. I thought, perhaps, men were all alike.'

Here she came into his arms, and perhaps cried a little, but he could not see her face.

'And you won't believe things about me again which represent me in the light of an utter beast and an abandoned liar?'

'No, never again! I'll trust you all my life, dear.'

'Well, I must be off now. Good-night, my love—you do love me, don't you?'

'I do. That's an old story now.' And soon he went.

Nora remained where she was. She just heard his step on the swept, hard-frozen gravel pathway, and then heard him suddenly say :

' What the devil do you want ?' in a loud voice.

She looked through the window then, drawing the blind to one side, and saw him distinctly, in the bright moonlight, lying on the snow which covered the grass lawn alongside the gravel approach. She opened the drawing-room window and jumped straight out, without waiting for extra covering of any kind, and went to him. She found red blood on the snow, and said :

' What is it ? Speak to me, my darling !'

A weak voice replied : ' I don't know. Some — idiot — practising lessons in massacre.'

' Dick !' rang out her voice clear and strong through the frozen silence. And she held Cunningham's head in her lap, sitting there in the snow, regardless of risk, in a thin black evening dress with an open neck. Dick came, and she said :

' Somebody's killed him.'

'Mercy! What next?' said Dick, and took up Cunningham in his arms and carried him into the house, into the dining-room.

'Here, Nora, put a lamp in the spare room, and light the fire, and tell Malone to go all he knows for the doctor.'

Nora went with a pale face and wild eyes, and blood and snow on her dress and arms and neck.

CHAPTER XXXI.

NORA SCANLAN sat one afternoon, very shortly after the late events, in an armchair, watching Cunningham in the bedroom where he had been laid. She sat there nearly all day and all night now. Very improper, was it not? Quite of a piece with all the other wild, undisciplined irresponsibility of these strange Irish, whom it has taken the great English nation five centuries to learn to thoroughly misunderstand. Love and hate actually guide them more than propriety, logic, or even law. It is very sad.

And she sat there, and through the sorrow laid upon her shone the enduring strength of love, which can work like a horse or a navvy, and feel no fatigue, and simulate cheerfulness and confidence when it feels the agony of anxiety and doubt; and she listened with wet eyes to the wonderful raving chatter of a fever-stricken man, telling in disjointed nightmare fragments all the history of his life, the underlying ground-truths of his nature.

Those delirious discourses of his laid bare the man's personality to her as his sanity had never done, and yet this innocent and high-hearted woman heard nothing which lessened her respect and love for him. His talk ranged from childhood to college days, and from them to maturer manhood; sometimes it was playful, sometimes scornful; sometimes he repeated fragments of verse in different languages, sometimes worried himself for an hour 'flooring' some imaginary examination paper, and often carried on conversations with persons and on subjects to her unknown; but in none of these involuntary and defenceless confessions was there aught revealed for which he need take shame.

When a man is delirious, it is, as a rule, injudicious to allow his girl to listen to what he says ; but in this particular case no harm came of it, rather increased the love and tender pity as of a mother for an inarticulate baby who is suffering and cannot tell her how, or understand why she cannot take away the pain she would willingly bear for him.

Perhaps the most trying feature of it all, though, of course, an extremely common one in such cases, was that he very seldom seemed to fully recognise who she was, but kept addressing her as all kinds of different people. Once he said :

' It is very kind of you to sit here and talk to me ; and you must find it an awful bore to look after a man who has had his legs and back paralyzed. You know I was run over by a railway train—a big, white goods train, all full of snow, tons of snow ; and the specific gravity of snow is no joke, when it goes over your spine. But you know that, of course—you nurses are so scientific in these days.'

He had the idea that he had been in a railway accident, and was in a hospital. He went on :

'Do you know, if you will allow me to say so, you remind me of a girl I used to know — in Venice. On the Rialto ; not many a time and oft, but once.'

'Oh, chummy, don't you know me ?'

'Eh ? Oh yes, I know you. Dear me, you don't think I'm delirious, do you ? I know you, of course. An excellent and most kind lady. I have not the pleasure of knowing your name, though ; but that which we call a rose——I say, do you mind my singing something ? It's rather cheek, but it relieves my feelings, and you needn't listen if you don't like.'

And he laughed, and sang :

'" My love is like the red, red rose
That's newly sprung in June,
My love is like the melody
That's sweetly played in tune."

That's Scotch, you know. I'm Scotch too.

    ' "Till all the seas gang dry, my dear,
      And the rocks melt in the sun."

I tell you what it is, old chap : you don't half know what love means. With most of you boys it's a gratification of personal vanity—something to show off about, and you're not happy till you've let everybody know what a pretty girl it is ; and all you want is to exaggerate her love for you, and minimize yours for her. I know something of it, too ; but there, that's no business of yours.

    ' "Ich hab' dich geliebet, und liebe dich noch,
      Und fiele die Welt zusammen,
      Aus ihren Trümmern steigen doch
      Hervor meiner Liebe Flammen."

Do you understand that, nurse ? That's German ; it means :

    ' " I loved you before, and I love you still ;
      Though the joints of the universe sever
      And sunder, the flame of my old love will
      Rise up from the ruins for ever."

I don't mind telling you a wise word or

two these hobby-horses may not hear. You are discreet and kind. I did love a girl once—and I love her now. I think she would be sorry if she saw me here, don't you?'

'I know she would,' replied poor Nora, with the tears standing in her deep true eyes.

Then Dick opened the door gently and beckoned to her.

'I'll be back soon,' she said to Cunningham, and followed Dick out of the room.

'Jane's here,' he said, 'and wants to see you. I'll stop with him for awhile.'

'I'll go down and see her,' replied Nora, wiping her eyes. 'Oh, Dick, he goes on talking and talking, and he won't know me.'

'I know. I've seen lots of 'em like that. But he'll live to thank you yet. Dr. Hanlon's after telling me he has a splendid constitution, and has every chance of pulling through.'

'Well, I hope so. If God takes him, Dick, I'll pray I may die too.'

And she went downstairs to see Jane
Smalley, who, after making inquiries, said :

'And you've no idea who did it ?'

'Not an idea. I saw nobody, and he,
poor dear! can only talk nonsense, and thinks
a train ran over him.'

'Well, I am in trouble too. That man's
coming this afternoon to settle with Johnny
about this wretched money, and I was depending before upon poor Mr. Cunningham
to help us out of it, and he has all the
information and everything, and I don't
know what to do. And whatever is done
must be done soon.'

Nora thought awhile, and then said :

'Now, listen while I tell you. You go
as fast as you can to the old man on the
hill. He knows a great deal more than we
do about something or other in this, and he
will help you. He likes you, and he likes
Johnny, and he told Mr. Cunningham
things. It's the only thing I can think
of.'

'Well, I'll try ; but it's awfully hard to

have to do all this without any help. I believe Scheiner tried to murder Mr. Cunningham.'

' But you told me he was dining with
Johnny, at the Club, at the time.'

' Then *she* did it.'

' But that's nonsense! Why would
she ?'

' Well, I suppose it is absurd. Then, I'll
go.'

And the valiant little girl set off again
along the road through the thawing slush,
while Nora went back to sit through the
slow torture of her lover's wandering words.
It is a common enough thing, and happens
to many, but it nevertheless is equally new
and bad to each, and one of the most pitiful
things among the many sorrows of the
world.

Dick, after hearing what Jane had under-
taken to do, said :

' I can't let the poor girl go up that bitter
hill and through all that business alone by
herself. There will be trouble, and there

may be a bit of a row. I'm going with her. I'll not be long.'

'Very well, Dick; you go. But come back soon.'

And his long legs soon helped him to overtake Jane, who said :

'I didn't like to ask you, but I'm so glad you've come. You'll come home with me too, won't you ?'

'I'll see you through, don't you doubt, now. I know a deal more about Mister Scheiner than he'll like.'

About this time, the Scheiners were taking afternoon tea at Fernbank, and responding suitably to Mrs. Smalley's remarks and suggestions about 'this dreadful affair of poor Mr. Cunningham.'

Mrs. Smalley could not help thinking that Mrs. Scheiner looked very ill, and rejoiced to hear that she was going to London to see her doctor.

'I am afraid you have found our winter here rather trying,' she said ; 'and you don't look quite as strong as we could wish.'

'Oh no!' said Kitty. 'I am not as strong as I could wish.'

Hélène was present. Lilian was engaged with a bilious headache, and Florrie was reading a story-book before the schoolroom fire. Florrie was shy of visitors, and silent before them, and devoted to story-books. It was proposed that a little tea and conversation should precede the time when 'you gentlemen will want to go into the library to talk business.'

Mrs. Smalley was very dignified and graceful in her widow's attire, and gave the impression that she appreciated its becomingness, and regarded widowhood distinctly in the light of an added dignity.

'Such an extraordinary thing, too, this scandal about Mr. Cunningham! You have heard of it, of course, Mr. Scheiner?'

'That he has a wife and family in town? Oh yes, I have heard of that. It is perfectly appalling!'

'One does not like to say such things when the poor man is, so to speak, at

death's door; but they do say he was pay-
ing attention to Nora Scanlan, my niece,
you know.'

'I have some reason to suppose that
that, however regrettable, is true.'

'Such a dreadful thing, too, and a clergyman's nephew and all! And I have heard,
at least Mr. Paynter told me, that he has
been married for years to quite a low
woman. And we never knew anything
about it!'

'Mr. Paynter is usually accurate,' replied
Scheiner; 'it is his strong point.'

'I always say it comes of young men
living alone in chambers in London; they
fall into all sorts of temptations, and into
designing hands. I am so glad my Johnny
has given up that life. A young man is
so much better and so much safer in the
pure atmosphere and nice occupations of a
nice English home in the country.'

'Such as this. You are indeed right,
madame.'

'I am afraid Mr. Cunningham's society

can have had no good influence on him, and I am really thankful that kind of life has been quite given up.'

Hélène was chatting her usual trivialities to Mrs. Scheiner, who displayed as much interest as she could, but really felt physically weak and far from well, and looked it, in spite of the artificial means, external and internal, she had used to give herself the appearance and demeanour of a cheerful woman at ease with her surroundings. Leo had insisted on her accompanying him, in order, as he gracefully said, that the trap might not fail at the last moment for want of bait.

But something Hélène said had at last the effect of really interesting Kitty. It was this :

' Do you know, Louisa, one of our servants, a rather nice girl, says that she was out that evening to post a letter, according to her account, though the post certainly does not lie in that direction.'

'Something did, apparently,' murmured Leo.

' Yes ?' said Kitty, leaning forward.

'And she thinks she saw a woman running in the road. And mamma says perhaps this wife of Mr. Cunningham might have done the crime, followed him down here out of jealousy, you know.'

'Followed him—out of jealousy?' said Kitty, with a strange pallor showing round and through the *vinaigre rose de toilette.*

' Yes. You never know what these low women are capable of.'

' Never,' replied Kitty.

'I do not think it is exactly nice to repeat things the servants say,' said Mrs. Smalley. 'You are making dear Mrs. Scheiner quite ill, talking about such dreadful things. I dare say Louisa saw her own shadow, and that it is all nonsense. Let us talk about something pleasanter.'

Whereupon they all proceeded *not* to talk about something pleasanter, and Kitty had a 'pretty sick time ' until Johnny came in, and created a diversion by taking her conversation entirely to himself, soon after which some voices were heard in the passage, and Jane came in, followed by Dick Scanlan.

' Hullo, old man !' said Johnny. ' Patient no worse, I hope ?'

' No worse, but he can't talk sense yet ; and when he does it's even betting he doesn't know what happened to him.'

' Did you or Miss Scanlan,' asked Kitty Scheiner, with a dry mouth and giddy brain, ' see nothing at the time ?'

' Not a thing.'

' Ah, what a pity !'   And she felt more tranquil.

' Why don't you shut the door, Jane ?' said Mrs. Smalley.   ' You're letting in a frightful draught.'

Jane made no reply, but laughed, and her eyes sparkled with mischief.

A noise was heard in the passage, as of someone clearing his throat with unrefined emphasis.

' Who is that ?'

' Oh—I don't know—I'll see.'

And Jane left the room. Then there was a ring at the bell. Jane opened the front-door, and shortly after ushered in Mr. Paynter.

' Oh, how-de-do ! I say, who's that old chap in the hall ? What is he after ?'

' Won't you take some tea, Mr. Paynter ?' said Hélène.

' Thanks, yes. I don't mind if I do. I say, Scheiner, your wife's been lookin' awfully ill lately. I think you really ought to do something.'

' I'm going to do something,' replied Leo, with a smile.

Jane came in again, this time accompanied by a withered, shaking old man, in a pilot coat too large for him, holding in his hand a tall hat of ancient date, so as to expose its inexpressibly filthy interior. A marvellously aged man, with a parchment-yellow bald head, bristly cheeks and chin, toothless, save for his canines upper and lower, glassy eyes, and a brown viscous streak of tobacco at each corner of his mouth. It was the old man from the hill, much older and feebler since his accident— an awful old man, like a dead man in whom galvanism has established the feeble semblance of life. But he was not dead. Oh, not at all ! And he was accompanied by a rummy exhalation. Scheiner gasped, and rose, and sat quickly down again.

'What is the meaning of this ?' asked Mrs. Smalley, with suitable majesty. 'Why do you not go to the back-door if you want anything ? The Back Door !' she repeated louder.

'I bain't sa deaf but what I can't year, mum,' observed the recluse ; 'an' I come in at the front-door 'cos my pretty yer ast me !'

'I say, what do you want, old chappie ?' said Johnny good-naturedly. 'You know me. Is anything wrong ?'

'Yes, there be summat wrong. Yer, you listen to me, Johnny Smalley. You be

goin' to sell some o' that ere prap'ty over
to Parchmith, bain't ye ?'

'If you must know,' said Johnny,
humouring him, ' I was thinking of doing so.'

' To this yer Partygee ? So I yeard.
Now, I object.'

' Is he off his head ?' murmured Johnny.

' No, I bain't off my 'ed. It be meddlin'
hold, my 'ed, but it 'ave got summat in it.
That 'ere be my prap'ty, and I bain't goin'
to 'ave 'ee sold. 'Specially to Jumper.'

Johnny looked at Scheiner, who was
green, and fiddling with his fingers and
muttering.

' Who do you think you are, then, you
old maniac ?' pursued Johnny.

' There bain't no think about it. I knows
'oo I be, and I can prove it. An' Passon
Gilchrist 'ee knows, too. You ast 'ee. I
be John Smalley, coxswain's mate aboard of
his Majesty's ship *Victory*, Hadmiral Lard
Nelson. And I bain't mad, no more nor
you be. I was barn in the parish o' Yarmouth, Isle of Wight, in the year seventeen

'undred and heighty, kursened in the parish
church, and it's in the books. You ast
Passon Gilchrist. 'Ee've got my papers ;
'ee 'ave my baptism, my marriage at
Parchmith, the birth o' my two children,
an' all. An' why 'ave 'ee got 'em ? Because I give 'em to 'ee. Johnny Smalley,
and Mr. Scanlan there, I be your great-
grandfather ; and I say that be my prap'ty,
an' I won't 'ave 'ee sold.'

' Is this raving, Dick, or not ?' said
Johnny, grasping the back of a chair and
perspiring.

' It is quite true, to the best of my knowledge,' replied Dick. ' It is also true that
that Scheiner there had the honour of
sharing six months at the same Quane's
Hotel as our great-grandfather, who has seen
trouble, on one occasion. He was known
in the circles he then adorned as Jumper,
because—well, because he jumped, I suppose.'

' Do you believe the lies of a drunken
old ruffian like that ?' said Scheiner sullenly.

Dick turned on him quickly :

'Then, what price Alessandro Pellegrini and Miss Lily Goldstein, not to say Leopold Scheiner, me exalted nobleman ? It's all up, sonny, I tell you !'

Leo made a dash for the door, but Dick caught him and held him.

'Now, don't be struggling, or I'll have to hurt ye,' observed Dick, giving a gentle twist to the unfortunate alien's arm.

'What does all this mean ?' asked Mrs. Smalley, in alarm and anger.

'It manes,' said Dick, 'that this little girl with the golden heart and the clever head, and this old man, who is Johnny's and my great-grandfather, have saved you all from giving yourselves away, one way and another, to a cruel black-minded thief, and that we were not a minute too soon. Cunningham can give you proof of all this ; so can others.'

'Oh, I say ! Oh, my goodness !' said Paynter.

Johnny turned to her whom we must for the last time call Mrs. Scheiner, and said, with a dry sob :

' Is this true ? Did you know your husband was planning a fraud on me ?'

Kitty made no reply.

Leo laughed savagely, and said :

' Husband, too ! This boy is the best part of the entertainment this diverting afternoon has provided. You gave me away, of course, Kitty ?'

Kitty made no reply.

' What will I do with him, Johnny ?' said Dick.

' Let him go to the devil ! Turn him loose. He has not done me any harm.'

Scheiner was released, and went. As Kitty followed, she said in a low voice :

' Will you forgive me, Johnny ?'

He looked at her.

' I don't know. I have an idea you have broken my heart.'

And the two frauds left the house, Florrie, Lilian (bilious headache and all),

the servants, Mr. Paynter, and the rest of
the party watching.   Mr. Paynter said :

' Oh, I say !   Goo'-bye.'

And he hurried away to spread the news.
The old man remained where he was, and
nodded his head a good deal.   Johnny
turned to Dick, and said :

' That man gave himself away.   If he
had not looked in such a funk and tried to
bolt, I would scarcely have believed it.'

' Do you mean to tell me,' said Mrs.
Smalley, in a curious mixture of wrath and
terror, ' that that woman, whom we have
been receiving as an intimate friend, confidential with the girls, and going into society
here, is—is——'

' It appears, on her own admission, that
she is,' said Johnny dryly.

' Oh, what *will* people say ?'

' They're all in the same boat,' said Dick
consolingly.

' Are you quite, *quite* sure of what you
have said about him ?' pursued Mrs.
Smalley.

'Did he contradict it?' replied Dick.
'Did he carry on like an innocent man?
Didn't he completely lose his head directly
our relation here showed his face?'

The old man meditatively observed :

'Jumper, 'ee 'ave paid me a matter of
two pound a week to keep quiet for the
last six months.'

Mrs. Smalley turned to look at him, and
shuddered.

'Won't you sit down?' she said.

For all her little conventionalities, and
her shock and confusion, Mrs. Smalley was
a lady.

'Thank you kindly, mum ; I will.   It be
a meddlin' 'ard job for a hold man like I to
walk down Romer Down and back.   I be
ter'ble shook up sense I was throwed over
quarry.   I be gettin' hold, I specs.'

'Getting old!' said Johnny, with a hollow
laugh ; 'oh dear no!   Approaching maturity.
When did you say you were born?'

'I was barn in the parish o' Yarmouth,
Isle o' Wight, in the year seventeen 'undred

and heighty. I was boy aboard the *Triumph*, Captain John Darcy, at the battle off Ushant, Glorious Fust o' June, seventeen-ninety-four, Hadmiral Lard 'Owe. I can tell you the names of most of the ships in the fleet I've served in; I can tell you the names of most of the ship's companies aboard the ships where I served. And I can't read a word of print or writin'. That'll show you whether I be telling you a lie.'

At this moment a carriage drove up, and a footman jumped down and pealed at the bell.

Jane watched through the conservatory, and exclaimed :

' Good gracious ! It's Lady Gooch !'

Mrs. Smalley sat down, and her spirit broke, and she wept. That the Gooches should call at last, and select such an occasion ! To find this dreadful old man here, who said he was a relation, and it might be true—the original of that heroic but misleading family portrait in the dining-room, ' Captain ' John Smalley.

But relief came.   Lady Gooch and the Misses Gooch were content to leave cards, without even asking if Mrs. Smalley were at home, and then the long-tailed, white-headed footman climbed up to his box, and the carriage crashed and rolled proudly over the gravel to confer the glory of its presence on some other family.   The fact was that Lady Gooch had made up the extraordinary organ she called her mind that Mrs. Smalley ought to be called on, not because her friendship was desirable, or her social rank entitled her to such treatment from a near neighbour, but because her husband was dead.   It is also true that Johnny Smalley was well off now, and a bachelor, and that Lady Gooch had two tall, thin, long-necked daughters ripening on her hands ; but, to do her justice, Lady Gooch did not dwell much on the mercenary side of the question.   She really believed she was doing a kindness in leaving two large cards at Fernbank without expressing the slightest desire to see the inhabitants of that house.

Hélène took her mother away, and the two young men, Johnny and Dick, were left with their Common Ancestor.

' I must be off,' said Dick ; ' I promised to be back soon.'

' I suppose, old chap,' said Johnny to him, ' that you have done me a great service among you, and that I have been an immense fool ; but I don't at present feel quite as grateful to you as I might. You know the thing the spirits sing in " Faust ":

> ' " Thou hast destroyed
> A beautiful world."

How does it go ?

> " We carry the ruins
> Away into nothing,
> And weep for the beauty
> Lost and destroyed."

Well, I feel rather like that. I am pretty fairly knocked out, and I'd like to be left alone for a time, until I can talk to old Cunningham again.'

' I understand. But what will we do with this—this Fragment of History here ?'

Johnny said to the old man :

'If your story turns out true—and I don't say it isn't, mind, only it's a trifle startling to have a deceased ancestor sprung on you, who says he's getting old at 107— you must come and live here, of course. I don't know in what light the law would regard the rights of a man to property which his heirs have legally inherited, but we can see that you are comfortable. We'll show you the family portrait.'

'No, Johnny ; I'll bide where I be, up Romer. I can see the ships go by, and you can see as I 'aves my grog and baccy served reg'ler, and I'll tell you some more stories. I be gwine 'ome.'

And he put on the tall hat and went away.

Well, the apparition of the Common Ancestor, and the exposure of Scheiner and the unhappy woman who was connected with his miserable career, practically bring this story to an end. All the people in it are, no doubt, doing and suffering all kinds of interesting things; but they are things belonging to other and unwritten stories.

When Leopold Scheiner got outside Fern-bank into the public road, he walked rapidly to the Riviera Hotel, his partner silently following, where he found a telegram waiting for him from Lord Croaghpatrick, at Waterloo Station, to the following effect:

'Two parcels just left by train.'

He noticed the time at which this had been handed in, and saw that there was no time to lose.

'Kitty,' he said, 'put everything you can into your bag. Crow wires that two detectives are on their way here. We will, I think, cheek our way out of this yet. But make haste, there will be a train soon!'

Soon afterwards this enterprising man calmly ordered a carriage to drive him and Kitty to the station. He gave the driver a gratuity as usual at the station, and directed him to order dinner for half-past seven for two when he got back to the hotel. Then he took two first-class single tickets to Waterloo, and the pair got into the train. At the next station, a small one, crowded with farming men who had been to a cattle-fair, they got out and bought different tickets separately for Westleigh, and entered, one a third-class smoking compartment, the other a second-class carriage for women only. Shortly after they had left Redcliff the local police-inspector bustled in and made inquiries. Then he wired along the line that a well-dressed man and woman, etc., etc., were travelling first-class with tickets to Waterloo. Consequently, the man sent to keep an eye on the train at the junction known as Westleigh reported that no two first-class passengers answering the description got out there, or were in the train, nor did any of the passengers who *did* get out have tickets for Waterloo.

Leopold Scheiner, as he observed of himself, was a good strategist. Moreover, he had taken the precaution, some days before, to draw all his money from the bank where he deposited it, in case of a sudden departure becoming necessary. In accordance with his instructions, Kitty ignored him entirely at Westleigh, and bought a second single to Southampton. He bought a third to the same destination, and they travelled thither in the same train, but in different compartments, as before, and as strangers to one another. They arrived at Southampton in the dark, and left the station separately, meeting together when they had got far enough from observation by officials. Then they went to a hotel and dined, and in the evening prowled about, endeavouring to ascertain if the Havre boat were watched. It was not, and in due course they went on board of her, again as strangers, and the boat started, and no one interfered with them. It was a dirty night, with a south-westerly wind and rain, and they were both direfully sick, but arrived at Havre safely. There they no longer kept up any pretence of being strangers, but went on together to Paris. There they invented a new alias, while Leo removed his moustache and altered the way of arranging his hair, and proceeded to live upon their savings, which kept them for some weeks. After that Leo did a little betting, but not very successfully, so they tried to pick up young Englishmen at *table d'hôtes* and sight-seeing places, and do the old decoy business, with varying success.

The shock and scandal at Redcliff at the manner in which the chaste, superior, and intelligent society of that summer resort had been taken in, swindled, victimized, and made hopelessly ridiculous, was something awful, and Cunningham enjoyed it thoroughly. It helped to accelerate his recovery. For he did recover, and said it was worth a journey to the edge of the Land of Silence and Darkness for the sake of the coming back again.

'I awoke,' he said afterwards, 'from a mad muddle of dreamy abominations, and the first thing I saw waiting for a sign of sanity in me was the face of the most beautiful woman in the world, and the best.'

'That's dear old Paddy, I suppose,' said Johnny.

'Yes ; there is no one else like her, and never was or will be. I believe she never slept till she'd saved my life.'

'*I've* awoke from a mad muddle of some kind, too, old chappie, but what I can't stand is the infernal jaw, jaw, chatter, chatter, and general worrit that goes on about it. It is as bad in the house as it is out of it. I tell you what, I shall just hook it. I shall go abroad anywhere where I don't see my neighbours' or relations' faces, or hear their tongues.'

'Good. I think I would.'

'Why not come, too ? It would do you good. Paddy will be glad to have you out of the way for a week or two, to rest, and go and buy frocks, and I don't care a cuss where I go as long as it's a good long

way from home.   And I want someone I
can bore and rant to, someone who understands the shibboleths of the inside track.'

' I'll see.   I'll make up my mind this
evening.'

' Going to take counsel's opinion at The
Oaks first, I suppose.   Gad, you're a lucky
beggar !   Who'd 'a thought it ?   Do you
remember once calmly telling me that you
thought conversation with Miss Scanlan
would be rather uphill work ?'

' If you will come a little nearer I'll kick
you.'

' Did she ever tell you she refused me ?'

' Of course she did.   I told her she was
a very sensible girl.'

The upshot of this was that Cunningham
and Johnny Smalley did go for a brief
ramble in the spring through Holland and
Belgium, and it happened, during their stay
in Brussels, that they turned to pass an
idle hour at one of the little *cafés chantants*
near the Gare du Midi, a humble place with
tables for, perhaps, three dozen consumers

of *brune, faro, lambic,* or *bavière,* where the performers carry round two thick white plates for subscriptions between the turns, emptying the coppers from the upper plate into the lower after each contribution, according to a professional superstition that if you do not see what the last person gave you may be induced to give more, or rather not to give so little, yourself.

And in a few minutes there came on the little stage a woman, in the usual brilliant-coloured short skirts (which had seen better days), black tights, and crimson satin boots, who, after finishing a glass of *bavière,* sang a song in French, with an archly-idiotic chorus of ' La, la, la, Lodoviska !' to an accompaniment which a man jingled and banged out of a piano.

' Great Scott !' said Johnny, ' it's Kitty Scheiner.'

It was. When she came down the room with the plates, not having noticed our friends in the general crowd, Johnny said :

'I say, I'm off to bed. I can't stand this.'

And he left the place.

'All right,' said Cunningham. 'I'll follow shortly.'

When she came to him, he bowed gravely, and put a twenty-franc piece into the plate. She poured it mechanically into the lower plate and stared at him. He said :

'Sit down, and take a glass of beer. You can spare a few minutes ?'

'Certainly. I have not to sing for another two or three turns.' And she sat down, still bewildered.

'I want to know,' he said, 'what you did it for ?'

'Have you told anybody ?' asked she, looking round nervously.

'No. I let them all think I don't know who did it. But I do know quite well. Only I don't understand. *Why* did you do it ?'

Lowering her voice to a whisper, she said :

' I did not mean it for you. I meant it for Leo. I mistook you for him.'

' The excuse really almost justifies you, I think. But he was not there.'

' That was my mistake.'

' And why did you want—ah, well, that's your business. I dare say you had good reasons.'

' I am very sorry,' she said weakly.

' For nearly killing one gentleman instead of another? Well, it is rather an awkward mistake, isn't it? But I say, Mrs. Scheiner—— '

' My name is Kitty O'Reilly.'

' Well, Miss O'Reilly, then. Next time you'll put it into the right man, won't you?'

' I dare say I may.'

' Where is he?'

' Playing the piano there. It's fortunate he has so many talents, is it not?' she said sarcastically.

' Any way, the present business is honest, if not highly profitable.'

'Honest ?   Oh, very !   We bite the crust of honest industry, and live on sausages and onions, and dirty salads and Belgian beer. Oh, there is nothing like honesty! So elevating and ennobling, too.   I am Miss Betsy Valkerr from London, and I sing "Lodoviska" first, then " The House where Charlie uses," and then if the audience are good, and fairly generous, I dance them a hornpipe.   Leo plays the piano all the time. If you will stay, I will dance to-night for you.   You are a gentleman such as not many are, and I would go on my knees and kiss your hand, if you would forgive my horrible folly.'

'That was only an error of judgment, an accident, almost.   What was much worse was the way you spoilt young Smalley's life, or nearly did.   At any rate, it was not for want of trying if you did not.'

'I did not know it would be so serious. I have been accustomed to act as decoy for a thief, and that blunts the finer feelings.

But I liked Johnny, and am sorry. My sorrow is of no use to anyone, not even to me, but it may be a satisfaction to you to know that I am being punished. I am sinking into lower degradation always, and when I get older, and my voice and appearance cannot be made by any means useful, I guess I shall be a beggar, live among common criminals and rag-pickers, and be pushed and ordered about by policemen. And when I am dead no one will know who I was, or care, and I shall be put underground with no name, at the public expense, in some town or other. Now I must go and sing " The House where Charlie uses." Don't you want to wait and see me dance? No? Then, good-bye. Merci, monsieur !'

Cunningham went away. He found Johnny at their hotel, taking a brandy-and-soda, and looking very wild and sorrowful.

' Well?' Then Cunningham told him what had passed. ' Let's go away from here,' said Johnny. ' It's horrible. You know, old man, I may just as well tell you, I haven't left off loving that woman. If I stay here I shall go fairly off what little " chump " I have.'

' Right. We'll be off to-morrow to the Rhine. Now, take a good big drink, and I'll join you, and then go to bed.'

That was the last seen or heard of the two adventurers. Johnny and Cunningham returned to Redcliff in the course of April, and the former lived much as usual. He avoided Redcliff society, save that only of Cunningham and the Scanlans, and in course of time regained much of his old cheerfulness. But he never was quite the same as before he met Kitty, and never will be.

The Common Ancestor is, I am informed, in reasonable health still, and his abode on the hill has been much improved. Mrs. Smalley has had the family portrait put away in the lumber-room. She is a little confused in her mind as to what has happened, but is approaching the conviction that she 'had always said so,' and 'never liked the people,' and 'observed something about them from the first.'

The story of Cunningham's reputed *mésalliance* has been explained to her many times, but she will never be got to believe that there was not 'something in it.' And all through this trying period it was a great consolation that Lady Gooch had left cards.

It is considered probable that Cunningham will draw the line at standing (even unsuccessfully) for a borough in the Home Rule interest; but there is no knowing what lengths he may not be led or driven to by that most sweet sovereign lady of his, still by some irreverently called Paddy.

One day in the month of May, when the sun was shining, and the sea still and blue, Jane, walking on the edge of the cliff, observed to Dick Scanlan, who was with her, the others being a little way behind :

'I am getting on with my romance. It

is very thrilling, but it doesn't always connect up very well. There's a girl in it like me.   And there's a man in it like you.'

'Is there, now?'

THE END.

BILLING AND SONS, PRINTERS, GUILDFORD.

www.ingramcontent.com/pod-product-compliance
Lightning Source LLC
Chambersburg PA
CBHW031346070726
47496CB00017B/1810